Church C can be

Murder

By

ANN SUTTON

Book 2
A Saffron Weald Mystery

©2024 Ann Sutton

No part of this book may be reproduced in any form whatsoever, whether by graphic, visual, electronic, film, microfilm, tape recording or any other means, without the prior written permission of the author and publisher, except in case of brief critical reviews.

This is a work of fiction. The characters, names, incidents, places and dialogue are products of the author's imagination and are not to be construed as real. The opinions and views expressed herein belong solely to the author.

Permission for the use of sources, graphics and photos is the responsibility of the author.

Published by

>Wild Poppy Publishing LLC
>Highland, UT 84003

Distributed by Wild Poppy Publishing

Cover design by Julie Matern
Cover Design ©2024 Wild Poppy Publishing LLC

Dedicated to Nicola Coupe

Style Note

I am a naturalized American citizen born and raised in the United Kingdom. I have readers in America, the UK, Australia, Canada and beyond. But my book is set in the United Kingdom.

So which version of English should I choose?

I chose American English as it is my biggest audience, my family learns this English and my editor suggested it was the most logical.

This leads to criticism from those in other English-speaking countries, but I have neither the time nor the resources to do a special edition for each country.

I do use British words, phrases and idioms whenever I can (unless my editor does not understand them and then it behooves me to change it so that it is not confusing to my readers).

Cast of characters for Church Choirs can be Murder

Ophelia Harrington - Twin sister of Imogen
Imogen Pettigrew - Widowed twin sister of Ophelia
Tiger - The twins' Alsatian dog

Members of the Saffron Weald Choir

Reginald 'Reggie' Tumblethorn - Village grocer
Harriet Cleaver - Wife of village butcher
Arabella Fudgeford - Village sweet shop owner
Prudence Cresswell - Vicar's wife
Agatha Trumble - Primary School headmistress
Celina Sutherland - Village librarian
Patricia Snodgrass - Post mistress
Algernon Wainwright - Local historian
Desmond Ale - Pub manager
Colonel Winstanley - Retired, head of village council
Douglas Horton-Black - Choir director
Archie Puddingfield - Baker
Simon Purchase - Village deacon
Matilda Butterworth - Choir organist, tea shop owner

Other characters

Gladys Horton-Black - Choir director's wife
Constable Hargrove - Local bobby
Inspector Southam - County police inspector
Reverend Cresswell - Village vicar
Septimus Saville - Church verger
Pierre Ancien - Antique dealer

Prologue

Under cover of velvety darkness, as owls hooted and bats squealed, two dark figures met by appointment in the shadows on the edge of Stirling Woods.

One of the people present unfurled a soft, black rag revealing a heavy silver offering plate that winked in the half-moon light. The other pulled an envelope out of a pocket and thumbed the edge of a stack of wrinkled pound notes.

"Fifty quid." The dubious money bearer fired a challenging stare at the nervous character holding the plate.

The jittery individual threw the rag roughly over the precious artifact.

"We agreed on seventy-five."

"You *demanded* seventy-five. This item will be hard to sell. Don't know how I'm going to offload it and get my money back. I'm taking *all* the risk. Might get caught." The black marketeer spit onto the dark ground. "Take it or leave it. No skin off my nose." The pound notes began the journey back to the pocket.

The shadowy figure holding the collection plate made a quarter turn as if to leave, then reconsidered.

A sigh. "Alright. Give it over."

The two exchanged their goods then melted into the inky night.

Chapter 1

Crash! Bang! Wallop!
Panic and vexation flooded Ophelia Harrington's face as she gripped the arms of the easy chair.

"You stay here. I'll deal with it," Imogen assured her twin sister.

The sisters had recently acquired a huge Alsatian dog whom they had re-named Tiger. He was collateral damage from the arrest of the owner, a murder suspect whose reign of terror had been brought to an end by the sleuthing talents of the twins. For Imogen, a dog lover, meeting Tiger was love at first sight. Not so much for her sister, Ophelia, who had agreed to take on the hound for a probationary period only, before deciding his ultimate fate.

Imogen's heart sank.

Since they had adopted him, Tiger had dug several unsightly holes in the garden, tipped over the kitchen waste bin and run off with Ophelia's underwear when she was taking in the washing from the line. Imogen feared he was pushing her sister to the limit.

Hand on the kitchen door Imogen took a deep breath.

Tiger was grinning amidst a variety of pots and pans whose copper bottoms were reflected in his expressive amber eyes, looking very proud of his work.

They had left the pans to dry on the draining board before going to bed and forgotten to place them on the pot rack that hung over the table after breakfast. The bouncing light of the morning sun must have tempted Tiger to engage.

"Nothing broken!" Imogen cried before picking up all the pans and checking for dents. One small saucepan had a tiny dimple but she could not be sure it wasn't already there before Tiger arrived.

Tiger pushed his furry nose into her legs and Imogen wrapped devoted arms around him, drinking in his doggy scent. She and her deceased husband Wilf had owned dogs for most of their marriage and Badger's Hollow, her childhood home where she now lived with her sister, felt wonderfully complete with him there.

She went to the larder and found him a dog treat, directing him to lay on his bed.

"You mustn't upset Ophelia, or you won't be able to stay."

He tipped his head with questioning eyes and she felt her heart squeeze.

"Just a pan or two crashing to the floor," she explained as she returned to her book by the bare fireplace. "Nothing to worry about. Why don't you put on some jazz or practice the violin? Those things always make you feel better."

Ophelia let loose an enormous sigh then pushed herself up from the chair. Her violin case rested against the grand piano that sat in the light from the front window.

"How about you accompany me?" she retorted.

Ophelia was a skilled musician who had belonged to a professional orchestra for many years before retiring. Imogen was an average amateur at best. "Are you sure? I have trouble keeping up."

"No matter. It will be fun. Come on! It'll erase the shock from that clatter."

Ophelia chose some music, placing it on the piano's music ledge, then stood behind her sister as the photographs of their parents looked on from the mantle.

At first, Imogen's fingers had trouble finding all the right notes but eventually, her years of lessons kicked in and together they managed to play a decent duet.

"Bravo!" shouted a familiar voice through the open window. Tiger began to bark.

Pierre.

With surprising speed, Ophelia ran to the front door leaving her sister with a wry grin on her face. She was convinced there was some prior relationship between her twin and the handsome French antique dealer, though neither one of the pair admitted to it.

Sweeping into the room looking effortlessly elegant, Pierre crossed the space to kiss Imogen on the cheek. Why did she feel like giggling?

"I was not aware that you played the piano, Imogen."

"I took lessons for years as a girl, but I was never any good."

"You sounded pretty good to me," he contradicted.

"It was Ophelia's violin that made me sound better. She has the power to elevate others by the genius of her playing."

"Now, there I 'ave to agree." He sat on the sofa and twisted toward Ophelia. "I 'ave visions of you playing under the great oak on the village green on a late summer evening. Won't you do it?"

"I'll think about it," said Ophelia.

A scratching at the kitchen door reminded Imogen that Tiger was a social animal. "Excuse me. There's someone else who wants to see you."

Before she had even half-opened the door, the dog streaked through and into the lounge.

By the time Imogen returned to the front room, the dog was aggressively burrowing his snout into Pierre's side. Fortunately, Pierre was a dog person too, though he did not currently own one.

"Good boy," he crooned, chucking the dog's chin. After several seconds, Tiger placed his head on Pierre's lap.

Ophelia eyed the pair suspiciously.

"To what do we owe the pleasure of your visit?" asked Imogen.

"I was just passing. I try to stroll every day to keep the blood flowing. It's good for the constitution, as you English say. Since I'm 'ere, are you still enjoying the duchess's furniture?"

Upon returning to live in Saffron Weald the twins had purchased a duchess's cast-off furniture at Pierre's antique shop.

"It's luxurious! It was a marvelous choice," replied Imogen.

"Wonderful." He crossed his slim legs. "And socially? 'Ave you thought any more about joining a club now that you're settled?"

Ever since moving back to Badger's Hollow, the twin sisters had felt the pressure to fill the vacancy in the bellringer's circle, left empty by an unfortunate accident. Imogen was exempt due to an arthritic shoulder, but Ophelia did not want to join since Mildred Chumbley, head of the W.I., general bossy boots and gossipmonger, was the lead ringer. However, Ophelia was running out of excuses. It was time to decide on something else and quickly.

"I think the bell ringers are out," Ophelia admitted. "I can only take Mildred in small doses." She shuddered.

"What about the W.I.? They do a lot of good in the village."

"Same problem," said Imogen sheepishly. "I know mother was a member for years, but we're not inclined in that direction."

"There's always the bird watchers," he suggested. "I go out with them every now and again. There are splendid birds in these woods. Or, next year's fête committee." He snapped his fingers. "The theatrical society."

"So many options. We will try and decide soon," Ophelia assured him.

"You could always start your own," he said with a wink. "A musical or…puzzle society."

It was so brief Imogen almost missed it, but Ophelia had flashed him a warning. She must get to the bottom of this secret.

Chapter 2

A single ray of light shone through the stained glass, motes of dust spiraling in rhythm with the strains of the harmonious hymn, pinpointing the vacant spot in the church choir. It was as if God himself were pointing to the organization they should join.

Connie Featherstone, childhood friend of the twins and village librarian, had stood in that spot for over thirty years. Now she was in jail, having been convicted of murdering four people, including Ophelia and Imogen's elderly mother.

"I bet you can get out of the bell ringing thing if we offer to sing in the choir," Imogen whispered to her sister as they sat in the old pew of the gothic church.

Ophelia's lips pushed up as she considered the proposition.

"That might work," she replied.

"Let's talk to the vicar or someone, after the service."

The excellent choir provided the closing hymn and after the benediction the congregation ambled next door to fellowship hall for biscuits and coffee.

Prudence Cresswell, the vicar's stick thin wife, raised her hand to invite them to sit at her table.

"Wasn't that lovely?" remarked the celery-like Prudence in reference, they supposed, to her husband's sermon. "He spends so many hours getting the words just right." She touched a hand to frizzled hair that poked out from under a light green, felt hat.

"Certainly thought-provoking," agreed Imogen. The talk had centered on building one's faith on a firm foundation.

Prudence also happened to be a member of the choir. "Tell us what you think of Douglas," said Ophelia.

"Oh, are you interested in joining the choir?" asked Prudence as one of her children swung by the table and swiped one of her biscuits. She bestowed the errant child with an angelic smile. "I thought Bartholomew said you were going to teach Sunday School."

Right.

Their mother had taught Sunday School for decades and now that she had passed on, they had intimated to the vicar a willingness to accept the baton.

"Oh, yes. Now that we feel settled, I think we're ready to take on that responsibility," Imogen assured her. "But the choir wouldn't conflict with that assignment, would it? How often do you perform and practice?"

"The goal is to perform once a month but we practice most weeks on Thursday nights."

"Hello," said Alice Puddingfield, the baker's wife, plonking herself on the vacant chair at their table. She raised a biscuit. "What do you think? I tried a new recipe."

Ophelia took a bite. The confectionary treat immediately melted on her tongue with a rich, buttery flavor, filling her mouth with sugary comfort. "Oh, Alice, you're really onto something."

"I was just telling them about the choir," explained Prudence, the tendons in her neck like the prominent lines on a stick of celery.

"Are you thinking of joining?" asked Alice, whose husband also sang. "Archie loves it."

"Might be a good way to sink our roots back into the community," responded Ophelia.

"You mean other than solving the murder of your mother and three other people in your first month back in the village," retorted Alice with a snort.

"Yes, other than that," said Ophelia, chuckling.

Their mother's will had contained a recent codicil that required the sisters to live together at the cottage. In retrospect, it was their mother's way of making sure her murderer was caught. She had seemed to sense that her life was in danger and hid a notebook in the cottage she hoped the twins would discover and use, to find her killer. Which they did.

"Douglas knows his stuff," continued Prudence then dropped her voice. "And can be a bit of a stickler."

"Sounds right up my street," responded Ophelia. "I would appreciate working with someone who is a professional."

"Why are music people so snobby about it?" asked Imogen in a tight tone. "They use their prowess as a stick to beat down others. Not everyone can be an expert. I find it rather unchristian."

"What are you talking about?" asked Ophelia in surprise. "You read and play music perfectly well."

"I know, but I'm no expert. And that attitude would prevent the less talented from applying. Surely, it is the job of the gifted to improve the talent of the average. Not to become irritated with them." This was quite the soapbox speech for Imogen.

"*Flaming fiddles!*" said her sister with a campy smile. "Duly noted."

"Matilda Butterworth is the organist," continued the vicar's wife quickly, her pale eyes darting from side to side due to the uncomfortable tension between the sisters.

"Is she the one who runs the tea shop?" asked Ophelia. "I must confess, we haven't been in there yet."

"Yes," responded Alice. "Beautiful white hair and a mother duck manner."

"She's simply wonderful on the organ," said Prudence.

"You've convinced me," said Ophelia. "I think we'll give it a whirl because anything is better than the bells with Mildred."

Tiger greeted them boisterously at the door, whipping his huge, hairy tail against the walls of the narrow hallway.

"Alright, boy!" soothed Imogen, letting him slip past her and into the garden.

"Let's see what damage he's done today," muttered Ophelia, taking off her fashionable hat and jacket and making her way into the kitchen.

Fresh gnaw marks on the bottom of one of the decaying kitchen chairs betrayed the dog's morning activities, while they had been out worshipping. Fortunately, though the sisters had replaced most of the furniture in the cottage, they had not yet tackled the kitchen.

"Just as well it's all shabby," sighed Ophelia.

"Oh!" said Imogen, who had stepped into the kitchen behind her. "I shall go to the butcher first thing tomorrow and get him a bone to chew."

In spite of their gardener playing with the dog in the large garden while he worked, and taking him on the occasional walk, the dog was still madly energetic.

Fortunately, the scrumptious odor of the chicken that had been roasting while they were at church improved Ophelia's mood, and they both set about preparing the vegetables and basting the bird. They had invited Pierre to Sunday lunch.

"Pierre will take one look at this table and chairs and encourage us to buy more items from his shop," chuckled Imogen.

Peeling potatoes, Ophelia grunted, "Well, until Tiger has his chewing under control, I think that's a silly idea."

Rather than anger Imogen, the future tense of Ophelia's comment made her extremely happy. It would appear that in spite of his shenanigans, Tiger was working his magic on her sister. At that moment, he scratched the kitchen door. Imogen let him in and he covered her in sloppy canine kisses. Ever since he had come to live with them, Tiger had given the cottage a heartbeat she hadn't known had been missing.

Once his welcome had run out of steam, Tiger sat under the table as the sisters worked.

When all the vegetables were simmering, they made themselves a pot of tea and as they were pouring their second cup, Tiger jumped up and began to bark.

"Pierre must be here." Ophelia went to the door, Tiger following her, to find Pierre holding a bouquet of colorful flowers, looking pressed and fresh.

"Ophelia." He leaned over the dog who was wiping his nose on Pierre's trousers and kissed her cheeks.

"How lovely!" She accepted the happy blooms. "Follow me."

"Pierre! How wonderful to see you." He kissed Imogen's cheek and her skin glowed in response. "Have a seat." She took his hat and Tiger settled himself back under the table at Pierre's feet.

"I didn't see you at church," said Imogen, setting the table.

He wrinkled his charming nose. "I'm Catholic. I prefer Mass. I only attend here at St. Mary's at Christmas and Easter."

"Ah, that explains it." She placed a plate in front of him. "By the way, Ophelia and I have decided to join the choir."

Pierre's lips tightened and he closed one eye. "A better choice than the bellringers but I understand there is some friction in the ranks."

"Oh?" commented Ophelia as she placed a folded serviette beside each plate.

"Nothing more than is usual in any organization, I'm sure. And they do have a beautiful tone. They're one of the reasons I attend at Christmas."

"Prudence mentioned that Douglas Horton-Black is a real artiste," said Ophelia.

"That's one way to put it." He winked at Imogen whose stomach fluttered unexpectedly. She swallowed and spun to open the oven door and remove the chicken.

Good heavens, girl! You are sixty-five years old!

Ophelia watched the interaction between Pierre and her sister with interest and a whisper of jealousy.

"Perhaps you would carve for us?" she asked him.

"I'd be honored."

Once the chicken was cut, the vegetables dispensed into serving dishes and the wine uncorked, they all sat down at the table. Tiger placed his head on Imogen's feet.

"May I propose a toast?" Pierre asked.

The sisters locked eyes.

"Of course," said Ophelia with some curiosity.

"Thank 'eavens for the return of the Harrington twins!" Holding his wine glass aloft he bestowed a charming grin on the pair.

Imogen giggled and Ophelia smiled broadly.

"May I ask why we deserve such a toast?" asked Ophelia.

"Well, for one thing, you put a mad killer away and saved our village from a psychopath."

"That much is true," she responded.

"And for another, you have added some 'omegrown color to the village that I feared would be missing with the passing of your dear mother. You 'ave the power to shake things up a bit."

"To shaking things up!" declared Ophelia holding her wine glass up for them to clink.

Chapter 3

The one-story cottage Douglas Horton-Black shared with his wife, Gladys, and their black cat, Spartacus, was neat as a pin. The smell of pine and lemon betrayed the cleaning that had occurred before the arrival of the twins.

In his early fifties, Douglas taught orchestra and choir at the high school in Parkford. A child in grade school when the twins had left the village, his mother had been Ophelia's first violin teacher.

The well-kept sitting room was tastefully furnished in Queen Anne pieces with a prominent bookshelf containing old tomes, and the heavy, ornate fireplace bore record of the places to which they had traveled before Gladys's illness.

"Do sit down." Mrs. Horton-Black was not originally from the village. Douglas had met her on a fishing trip to Yorkshire and her accent was as fresh as if she had stepped off the train yesterday. Gladys had become a beloved infant teacher at the primary school and held the position for over ten years.

"I can't tell you how thrilled I am to hear that you want to join our little choir." On Douglas's narrow lap sat a pile of sheet music. "I've picked out a few songs for the audition that we've tackled in the past."

As he reached over to hand the papers to the sisters, Imogen felt a knot of nerves twist. This assessment was going to be a lot more vigorous than she had supposed. Glancing at the sheet of music, she let out a small breath of relief. It was a song she had sung years ago at school. Running over the notes on the page, she imagined herself playing them on the piano.

Ophelia appeared calm as the proverbial cucumber. This was her world. Her element.

The Horton-Blacks possessed the most beautiful grand piano. It gleamed so bright in the morning sun that Imogen had to shield her eyes.

Pulling on the crisply ironed crease of his trousers, Douglas sat on the piano bench, running lithe fingers up and down the keys in a show of proficiency. Ophelia noticed the pride shining in his wife's eyes.

He thundered a chord.

"Right. Let's begin, shall we?" His prominent forehead rippled in expectation. "Soprano? Alto?"

"I'm an alto and Imogen's a soprano," explained Ophelia.

"How interesting." His intelligent, hazel eyes twinkled behind prim wire spectacles.

Turning back to the piano, he played the introduction, and the sisters began, Imogen's voice trembling a little until they had finished the first two pages.

It was difficult to ascertain what Douglas thought, as he played with his balding head thrown back, eyes closed, thin lips forming a straight, impenetrable line.

"It's just an insignificant church choir," Imogen told herself as they neared the end of the piece. "No need to worry."

When they had finished, Douglas left his fingers pressed to the keys, the sound reverberating around the room, diminishing in volume incrementally.

Imogen glanced at Ophelia who was wearing that self-satisfied look she sometimes wore.

Who needed the silly choir anyway?

"Lovely." Douglas opened his eyes. "Imogen, with training you could be a soloist. Would you be interested?"

Imogen started. She had always deemed herself the inferior one when it came to music. "I-uh, well…"

Ophelia laughed, but not unkindly.

"The limelight is n-not really where I'm comfortable," Imogen finally stammered out. "But it means the world to me that you would think so."

He swung thin legs to the side and faced them. "The two of you will add significantly to the choir. Welcome to our little troupe."

Imogen felt ridiculously happy.

"Now that's over with, let me get you some tea," said Gladys. Struggling to her feet, leaning heavily on a cane, she disappeared.

"Have you considered putting on a recital?" Douglas asked Ophelia in the clear diction a teacher develops over time.

She smoothed the fine gauze of her pale pink skirt. "Pierre was just asking me the same thing. He had visions of me playing in the evening on the green."

"I agree. Perfect setting with the pond in the background. But I also thought an inside venue where…" he picked an invisible piece of lint from his vest "…I could accompany you."

As much as Ophelia relished performing, she was ready to play for her own pleasure and not for that of others. "Let me think it over and I'll get back to you."

He clasped knobbly hands around his knees. "Of course."

"How long have you been the choir director?" asked Imogen.

"Going on twelve years now. The old chap died and since there was an upcoming performance, the former vicar asked me to step in because of my experience. The rest, as they say, is history. It makes a nice change to work with adults when you're used to working with excitable children all day." He cleared his throat. "I'd like to thank you for finding that young woman's killer, even though it left us shocked and dismayed to discover that the murderer was hiding among us in plain sight. A person we knew and trusted. And to think she did away with your wonderful mother, too!"

"Not only that, she had the cheek to keep cozying up to us." Imogen fingered the gold locket at her neck. Though usually of a mild temperament, this was a topic that really riled her.

"Douglas!" called out Gladys.

"I'll just go and help with the tray," explained Douglas, leaping to her aid.

They returned with a tray laden with goodies and the conversation turned to Doug's life as a teacher.

Arriving at the church five minutes before practice was due to start, the twins found that most of the choir members had already assembled.

Colonel Winstanley shook their hands. "So good to see you. We just didn't sound quite the same missing a soprano." He refrained from alluding to the reason for the void.

Reggie sent them a small wave from the choir stalls. Wearing a chartreuse shirt paired with light blue trousers, he seemed a little out of place in the conservative sanctuary.

"How lovely!" he declared. "A true musician among us."

Desmond Ale, portly owner of the public house, arrived puffing and mopping his brow, along with Simon Purchase, the young church deacon.

"Come up here," beckoned Prudence Cresswell to Imogen. "It's where you-know-who used to stand."

Imogen stepped up and stood between Arabella Fudgeford and the vicar's wife.

Douglas arrived from behind the altar carrying stacks of music which he handed out as the local historian, Algernon Wainwright, wobbled his way up the aisle.

Taking a surreptitious glance at the sheet music, even Ophelia thought the choice of music challenging for a parochial choir. Fortunately, again, it was a piece with which Imogen was already familiar.

"Sorry, I'm late!" gasped the new librarian, Celina Sutherland, her fine, black hair flying out from her rosy face. She jostled herself into place among the altos.

Presiding over the small choir with the authority of a symphonic maestro, Douglas pushed the wire glasses up his narrow nose, sharply tapping the music stand with his ivory baton.

"Let's commence with our jaw exercises. And begin."

Imogen looked helplessly around as the other choir members shifted their jaws into various unnatural positions. She felt the urge to snicker but held herself in check. Not even the colonel complained.

"Scales!" Douglas barked, while fiddling to organize the music on his stand with a small clip.

Matilda Butterworth, whom neither twin had yet noticed, ran them through a difficult set of scales on the organ that certainly exercised the voice.

"Open your choir folders."

No one else seemed bothered by the director's brusque manner.

"This magnificent hymn will serve as the capstone of the Harvest Festival service," he explained, running a tongue over dry lips. "Let's give it a run through." Arms raised and taut, he flicked the baton like a switch, pointing it directly at the sopranos as if he were a wizard putting a hex on them.

After a slightly rocky beginning, the choir members found their stride and made a respectable run for the finish line. Imogen held her breath. Douglas was obviously a perfectionist but his undeniable talent had clearly earned the respect of the other choir members.

"Not bad, not bad. Matilda, let's take the parts separately now that we are familiar with the tune. Please play the soprano line only."

Imogen rocked from side to side. They had been standing for over half an hour and her legs were beginning to prickle. Douglas pierced her with a look so sharp, she stopped abruptly. Sandwiched between two of the tallest women in the village, Prudence, whose high voice was wobbly like a warbler, and Arabella Fudgeford, the young proprietor of the *Jolly Lolly* whose tone was smooth and rich, Imogen tried to ignore the discomfort in her veins.

Agatha Trumble rounded out the sopranos with a strong operatic voice. Agatha was a horsey woman in her forties who had begun her working life as the year two teacher at the Saffron Weald primary school fifteen years before, working her way up the ladder to become the headmistress. In spite of the glamor her title might suggest, the school was small enough that out of necessity, Agatha was involved in all the behind-the-scenes workings of the school, from repairman to head bottle washer. However, her reputation as a firm but fair leader was well deserved. This was the closest Imogen had ever been to the woman who bore a teeny, star shaped birthmark on her jugular notch.

Imogen peeked over at the alto section to gauge whether her sister was experiencing the same aching in her legs and caught

Celina's eye. She was a pretty, young woman who had been promoted to head librarian in the wake of the arrest of her boss.

"Douglas, can we go over *our* notes?" asked Patricia Snodgrass, the post mistress who fit the mold of librarian much better than Celina.

"Yes, I need to hear it again," said Harriet Cleaver, the butcher's wife, who made up the final member of the lower women's section.

"Of course!" Douglas tapped the stand again. "Matilda! Alto part. One, two, three and four."

After practicing several times, he ordered Matilda to play the tenor line. Reggie, Algernon and Archie sang out the notes with reasonable accuracy.

The basses were next. Desmond, the colonel and Simon, rendered the part with a profound richness that managed to earn the praise of the exacting conductor.

With expert precision, Douglas unified them all in another run through. Imogen thought it a vast improvement on the initial offering.

"Stop!" cried out the choir director suddenly as if warning an engine driver to slam on the brakes because a bridge was out. He pierced the air with the baton in the direction of the tenors. "Someone's off."

This was exactly the kind of treatment Imogen feared, called out and humiliated in front of the whole choir. The bones of her ribcage froze.

"Reggie, I believe it's you," declared the director with narrowed eyes. "You're singing b instead of b flat."

Rather than blushing more crimson than his outrageous shirt, Reggie nodded.

"And Agatha, blend dear. Blend. Now, let's take that again from measure fifty-two, and…" The baton waved and the organ played. "Much better," Douglas called out over the singers.

As they approached the ending, Douglas shot his baton into the air, elbow up, nostrils tight, as the sopranos hit the final high 'c'.

The very stone of the church walls trembled with emotion.

Douglas remained still, baton raised, eyes closed in apparent ecstasy. No one moved an inch. Imogen slid her eyes to the left, but Prudence was still as a statue, choir book held aloft.

Finally, Douglas dropped the baton and the choir members moved as if turned on by an electric current.

A single set of hands applauded the performance and Ophelia looked past Douglas to see the verger, Septimus Saville, his whole face pinched with exquisite joy.

"That will do for today," said Douglas. "Thank you, everyone. I'll see you at our next practice."

Imogen's whole body relaxed.

"Is he always this particular?" she whispered to Arabella.

"Oh, yes! We all know the rules and Douglas expects us to play by them. Strict adherence to the smaller things prevents larger problems—like chatting." She winked.

After the rigorous audition, yet pleasant visit at Douglas's home, Imogen supposed his choirmaster act must be a persona that he put on and off like an article of clothing.

"Wasn't that fun?" gushed Ophelia as they stepped down from the choir stalls. "I wasn't sure about joining the choir but it has turned out to be an excellent suggestion, Imogen."

They headed down the center aisle and out into the pleasant warmth of the late summer evening following Agatha Trumble and Patricia Snodgrass, who angrily swept a sapphire blue, silk scarf over her shoulder. Their body language seemed to suggest a heated discussion and the words 'humiliated' and 'take advantage' reached Imogen's ears on the light summer breeze. She raised inquisitive brows at her sister.

"Oh, don't mind them," said Harriet Cleaver coming up behind them. "Those two are always at loggerheads."

"Really?" asked Ophelia.

"Oh, yes! They're second or third cousins from a family from West Nibble that is plagued with intergenerational infighting. It all began before any of us were born. Do you remember a Charles Penworth and Roger Markam?"

"Yes. Schoolyard fisticuffs," remarked Imogen.

"Same family, just earlier editions. There was some dispute over an inheritance in the late eighteenth century or so I've heard."

"Could be time to bury the hatchet," commented Ophelia.

Harriet's head bobbed. "Yes, well, it's not going to happen anytime soon. See you, ladies. Welcome to the choir." She waved as she peeled off in another direction.

"Remarkable!" came a strangled voice behind them. "You both fit into the choir like a hand in a glove."

The slightly hunched verger in an ill-fitting suit, beamed. "I felt a certain *je ne sais quoi* with your voices added to the group. It was as though the choir was waiting for your return." He bowed and a vivid image of Uriah Heep flashed across Ophelia's mind.

As they reached the edge of the graveyard, his voice dropped, head spinning on his thin neck like an owl on the hunt. "I was more than a little impressed with your work in solving the murder at the village fête." His voice dropped further. "I was, uh, wondering if I might impose on you for a little matter that is, uh, causing me some concern."

Catching her sister's eye, Ophelia replied, "Well, that would depend, Mr. Saville. We are not professionals, you understand."

"That is the draw, frankly," he responded, running a hand down the back of his oiled hair. "It is a matter of some delicacy. Involving the police would only draw undue attention."

"How about you come for tea at around eleven tomorrow morning to discuss the matter?" suggested Imogen. "That way you can speak freely and we can decide if we have the ability to be of service."

"Splendid," he said turning the brim of his black hat in his hands. "Until tomorrow, then."

Chapter 4

Having discovered their mother's recipe book a few weeks after they moved into Badger's Hollow, Imogen was still trying to perfect her version of Beatrice Harrington's famous coffee cake. She had baked it several times, improving with each attempt. Today, in preparation for their meeting with Septimus, the comforting smell of the sweet delight crawled into every corner of the cottage, stirring up old memories like friendly phantoms.

While the cake was baking in their old oven, the sisters popped into their sprawling garden to weed and deadhead before the August sun became too stifling. Their gardener, Malcolm Cleaver, arrived after a while, to tackle the heavy stuff and play with Tiger.

Imogen sat back on her heels watching, as Malcolm threw a ball time and again for the deliriously happy dog. Contentment swaddled her like a comforting quilt. This was not the life she had imagined after Wilf died, but at this stage, she could honestly say it was much better. She was independent but not alone. Her children could visit as frequently as they desired but she was not yet a burden, a nightmare scenario that haunted the dusty corners of her mind.

A glance at her watch indicated that the cake would soon be ready and she signaled to Ophelia that she was going into the house. Finally exhausted, Tiger decided to follow, loping beside her and panting hard, while drooling all over her shoes.

Her daughter, Penelope, had been horrified upon discovering that the twins intended to keep the massive dog. Imogen had listed all the reasons why having a guard dog would be beneficial while explaining they had hired someone young and able to exercise and train the animal. Penelope had remained unconvinced.

But news of the dog had been overshadowed by the fact that her mother and aunt had succeeded in bringing a murderer to justice. Imogen smiled at the memory of Penny and her son

Fergus's scandalized faces. They had been vocal in their opposition to ladies of a certain age engaging in such a dangerous hobby as sleuthing. However, when the whole story was revealed in its entirety, and her children had learned that their beloved grandmother was one of the murderer's victims, they had changed their tune.

Opening the back door, Imogen allowed Tiger to enter first. His water bowl was almost empty and she swiped it from him while he searched her face with questioning, golden eyes.

While he gulped the fresh water, she removed the cake carefully, placing it on the center of the kitchen table to cool.

"I'm going to freshen up," she said to the dog. Wagging her finger she continued, "Don't even think about messing with that cake."

The gardener's brother, Peter, had recently painted her mother's old bedroom a gentle peach. Windows flung open, the summer breeze played against the sheer curtains, filling the room with the scent of the wildflowers on the garden's edge.

Glimpsing at her reflection in the dressing table mirror, Imogen noticed a sheen of perspiration glistening on her brow. Moving to the small bathroom, she wrung out her face flannel and wiped the cool fabric over her forehead.

"TIGER!"

The strangulated tone of her sister's voice penetrated the floorboards like sharp knives and Imogen ran down the stairs, wet facecloth still in her grasp. Tiger's snout was covered in golden crumbs, a look of abject shame filling his striking eyes as Ophelia flailed her arms.

"Naughty boy," said Imogen but her heart was not in it. She should have known better than to tempt a hungry dog. "It's my fault," she said to her sister. "I ought to have put it at the top of the larder."

"What are we going to give the verger?" asked Ophelia, regarding the sorry remains of the coffee cake.

"We still have some of those biscuits you made a couple of days ago," replied Imogen.

"Well, I hope they aren't stale!" snapped Ophelia.

This disaster, added to the others, would walk back the progress Tiger had made in Ophelia's affections, for sure.

With a belly full of dread, Imogen took the dog's large snout in her hands and wiped off the crumbs with her face flannel while murmuring gentle warnings. Tiger licked her hands in appreciation. She, for one, was completely and utterly under his spell and was terrified of losing him.

"Now go and lay on your bed." She pointed to his wicker basket lined with a tartan blanket. He obediently curled up, worried eyes still on Ophelia.

Her sister could not hold in her irritation and snorts of breath like those from an angry bull flowed from her nose.

"My fault entirely," repeated Imogen. "Don't blame him."

It was time for distraction. Imogen sang the opening trill of the magic flute aria that was their signature tune.

As she had hoped, Ophelia's grumbling instantly transformed into a reluctant smile as she sang back the second line.

Imogen executed the third line perfectly and they both laughed, the tension diffused.

"I'll put on the tea and finish freshening up. You may want to wash up as well." Imogen flicked her head toward her sister while pointing to her own cheek, indicating a smudge of dirt.

Ten minutes later, both sisters had changed into light dresses. Ophelia was a modern dresser. Her frock, a modern, drop waist in lavender, showed off her slim figure. Imogen had never quite got the hang of dressing to make a statement, and her dress was a rather old-fashioned, cream and pink Edwardian style. However, they both dressed their silver hair in the same loose roll at the nape of the neck.

As they arranged the stale biscuits onto a plate and placed a cozy over the teapot, there was a knock at the door.

Tiger let out a sharp bark but at a glare from Ophelia, he quieted.

"At least Septimus is punctual," commented Imogen.

While Imogen took the tray into the parlor, Ophelia answered the door and ushered in the spindly verger.

"Do sit down, Septimus." Imogen pointed to one of the armchairs beside the fireplace while Ophelia offered him a cup of tea with one of the biscuits balanced on the saucer.

The official position of verger was *Protector of the Procession* and dated back to the Middle Ages. In those days, the verger did actually protect the ceremonial procession of the vicar from attack, with a stick. Today the job was more of an organizational position that involved preparing everything for worship services, welcoming parishioners to church and keeping the grounds tidy.

Septimus was a relative newcomer to the village. He had been taken on by the previous vicar some twenty-five years before. As such, he was not among the villagers the twins had grown up with, but they knew him from their frequent visits to their mother.

Perching on the edge of the seat, he asked after Imogen's family and Ophelia's musical career. After filling him in on all the details, his expression fell into serious lines.

"The reason I need to talk to you is..." He glanced around the room as if the walls did indeed have ears. "Various valuable items are disappearing from the church vault."

Whatever Ophelia had expected him to say, this was not it. She glanced at Imogen who was mirroring her surprise.

"The church has a vault?"

His forgettable eyes came alive. "Yes. Saffron Weald became a repository for sacred vessels and religious artifacts during the dissolving of the monasteries in the reign of Henry VIII.

"The monks would spirit away their hallowed treasures to avoid their confiscation by the Crown. It was a dangerous time when many monks were put to death, so the whereabouts of the treasures was often taken to the grave."

"I remember learning about all that in history. I had no idea some of the items had ended up here," exclaimed Imogen.

"The holy relics used in our weekly services are kept up in the vestry, but as verger, I am commissioned with being the protector of all the items in the vault as well. I've spent

28

years making an extensive and detailed inventory of all the church's treasures in here—" He pulled a brown leather ledger from his pocket.

"At first, I thought I might have misplaced a couple of silver candlesticks. I searched high and low for them but then another item went missing and another." He looked up, eyes brimming with earnestness. "Someone is stealing from the church."

"Do you have any idea who it might be?" asked Ophelia.

"Not a one," he said, slipping the ledger back into his pocket. "But I have concluded that items tend to go missing around choir practices."

"Are you intimating that the thief is someone from the choir." Ophelia held his gaze.

"I suppose I am." His already pale face drained of any color.

"Have you talked to Reverend Cresswell about it?" asked Imogen.

Rubbing the skin behind his large ears he began, "That's where things get rather sticky. My cottage is tied to the job. Without it, I'd be homeless. I'd rather not have to mention it to him and come under suspicion."

"Oh, I doubt the vicar would suspect you," said Imogen hotly. "He's a thoroughly decent chap."

"I agree entirely," said Septimus, slicing the air with his hand. "However, *he* would be required to report the theft to the bishop of the diocese and, how can I put it? He is not such an understanding fellow."

Ophelia put a finger to her nose. "Ah. I understand entirely. So, how do you think we can help?"

He swung open both hands almost swiping the teacup from his lap. "I heard how you investigated the death of that young woman who came to the fête, how you followed clues and came to the conclusion that it was the librarian. I'm hoping you might do the same for me." His expression of hope would have melted the hardest heart. "As a third party, your questions would raise less eyebrows."

Imogen blinked at her sister.

"Can you take us to the vault and show us exactly where the items are missing?" asked Ophelia, remembering how useful searching the scene of the crime had been in their first case.

Septimus hesitated. "Only if we are *extremely* stealthy. I don't want anyone to suspect that I know. The church has an expansive collection of treasures in its coffers and I doubt anyone less conscientious in their record keeping would even notice anything missing."

"I think we can manage that," said Imogen. "You go on ahead and we'll appear to be taking a stroll through the churchyard and meet you by the back door."

"Oh, thank you!" He jumped up and left.

The tea and biscuit lay untouched.

The crypt of the ancient church was cold, damp and dark. Perfect for the wealthy dead but not so much for the vitally alive. Spider webs decorated dark corners, and serious, blank stone eyes on sculptures seemed to follow them around the basement.

Taking out a large, iron key, the verger opened an arched door and stepped even further down. Switching on a single bulb barely made a dent, as it hung like a lone stalk of wheat in a field after a plague of locusts have feasted.

Once their eyes adjusted, Imogen and Ophelia gasped. Untold wealth lay beneath the church. The dark, narrow vault room extended far under the transept and the apse for about thirty feet. On each side, shelf upon shelf was bursting with jeweled communion cups, candlesticks, silver platters and countless other precious religious items. In contrast to the dimness of the room, even in the meager light, the silver and gold gleamed. Witnessing this trove of treasure the sisters realized that the decrepit lock was horribly inadequate.

They followed Septimus down a few stairs and into the back of the room where he stood aside, pointing. Even after careful examination of the shelf in question, Ophelia could see nothing obvious missing. It was a needle in a haystack situation.

She faced him with knitted brow as Imogen peered to take a look.

"See this stack of four platters? There should be five," he stated. "Number three is missing. And those small candlesticks? There are only six. There should be eight."

The verger's housekeeping skills were truly impressive.

"Who else has a key?" asked Imogen.

"No one. The vicar leaves that responsibility solely to me."

"And I take it the items in this back corner are not in current use?" commented Ophelia.

"No. We have finer and newer items. These are in retirement, so to speak."

"And you notice that things go missing around choir practices?"

"Yes."

"Well, that narrows it down, I suppose. Though I can't imagine anyone in the choir being a thief." Ophelia looked around.

"What did we learn from our first investigation, sister?" warned Imogen. "Anyone is capable of anything. Don't let your preconceptions cloud your views."

"Duly noted." The dimness was beginning to strain Ophelia's eyes. "Do you have a torch, Septimus? I think we'd like to have a careful look at the floor and the light down here is just not bright enough."

"Of course. I'll be right back." His soles crunched across the floor and scraped up the steps as he left them alone.

Imogen's mouth pulled into a frown. "It's a bit creepy down here."

"On that we can agree. But can you believe how much loot there is? A mighty temptation for any thief."

"But who would even know all this was down here?"

"Someone in need of money."

The tapping of footsteps above them proclaimed the verger's return. Within seconds his shadow appeared in the doorway and he bounded toward them, handing the torch to Imogen.

She swung the beam to the floor around the shelf. If there had been any footprints, their own shoes would have obliterated them.

"Shine it here, Imogen."

Ophelia crouched down and reached for something.

Imogen pointed the light at her hand. Between Ophelia's fingers was a drop of wax.

"Do you use candles when you come down here?" she asked the verger.

He pursed his lips. "Haven't for years. Not since we got electricity. Besides, I know where everything is and the light from the bulb is sufficient for me."

"But someone who was here without authority might not want to use the electric light," said Imogen. "A candle would be far more discreet."

"Can you hand me the torch, please?" Ophelia directed the light to the side of the shelf. It was the last ledge in the room and sat snug against the basement walls.

At first, Imogen could not see what had caught her sister's interest but as Ophelia moved aside, she saw a dusting of dirt on the floor.

"That's curious," she said.

"It certainly is," replied Septimus. "It's been happening for some months. I think we must have mice…or rats that are digging about in the ceiling and causing the mess. If you will excuse me, I'll go and fetch the broom."

"Can I have a go with the torch?" asked Imogen.

She walked to the shelves on the other side of the musty room and lit her way then stopped as a shadow caught her attention. Reaching across some jeweled crosses, her hands made contact with the shadow. *Fabric*. Pulling carefully so as not to overturn the other items, Imogen kept tugging until the whole thing came loose. She handed the torch back to her sister and shook out the cloth, dirt and dust cascading as it unfurled.

A brown, hooded cassock!

"That's how they got in without anyone noticing," declared Ophelia. "They disguised themselves as Septimus."

The verger reappeared at that very moment holding the broom and halted.

"Are you missing any clerical garb?" asked Imogen holding up the cassock.

"Not that I'm aware of." He reached forward and inspected the garment. "This has a hood. Ours don't. And I think it's brown. Ours are black." He held it up and more dirt fell from it. "Looks more like a monk's habit than an Anglican garment."

"But it wouldn't raise anyone's suspicions if it was seen around the church," said Ophelia.

"You're probably right, there," he agreed.

Ophelia snapped her fingers. "The theatrical society! I bet they have costumes like this."

"And at least we know how the thief is sneaking in." She paused. "Are there any secret passages?"

"Not that I know of and I've made it my business to know every inch of this church," he declared

Imogen was still wandering with the light having given the cassock to Ophelia. She let out a low whistle.

"A lighter!"

"Could be mine," said Septimus. "I indulge in a little pipe smoking from time to time."

Imogen brought the lighter to them. It was small and smooth with a four-leaf clover engraved on one side.

His lips disappeared. "That's not mine. But I'm surprised I didn't find it. You two are very good."

Imogen blushed in the dark room while Ophelia took the compliment in stride.

Using the flashlight, they examined the rest of the room but found nothing else.

"I should like to try the lock," said Ophelia.

"Try it?" he asked.

"Break in," she explained.

His jaw dropped. "Alright."

They all exited and the verger inserted the large key into the lock. Ophelia withdrew a hatpin. "Often locked myself out of my flat," she explained with a wink as Imogen frowned.

The medieval lock was far too big for the slim pin. "Hmmph. Have you got a knife or a thin piece of metal?" she asked him.

The verger's nose met his bunched lips. "Would a screwdriver do?"

"Perfect!"

He ran out again.

"He's going to sleep well tonight," said Imogen with a chuckle.

As they waited, the sisters looked around the silent crypt. Various Stirlings, the nobility of the area, were laid out in stone coffins with effigies on the lids. The only people who could afford such a thing. A tiny, grated window let in a sliver of natural light.

"Here you go," Septimus panted on his return, handing her the tool.

Ophelia slipped the thin steel into the old lock and twisted back and forth until the mechanism snapped open.

"Tada!" She pushed on the heavy oak door which creaked on its ancient hinges.

Footsteps clattered above them. The verger's features flooded with desperation.

"We'll hide in here," Ophelia assured him. "Come and get us when the coast is clear."

Chapter 5

Nose to nose the sisters pressed their ears to the thick vault door.

"Septimus! I was wondering where you were."

"Harriet."

Harriet Cleaver! The butcher's wife. What was she doing down here?

"I wanted to talk about the order of service for the Harvest Festival."

Or was that just an excuse to explain why she was in the crypt?

"Of course. Let's go up to my office."

The voices trailed away.

"Harriet is familiar enough with the crypt to come down here?" Ophelia's eyes were shining with theories.

"Perhaps most of the regulars are," Imogen pointed out. "Just because we weren't, we cannot draw the hasty conclusion that no one else knows about it. It could be common knowledge. They've all lived here for years and been an integral part of the church community. It's something we should ask Septimus."

The excitement drained out of Ophelia's features. "I suppose you're right, ducky."

They moved away from the door.

"Since Septimus wants to keep this little investigation a secret, I suppose we should stay in here until Harriet leaves," said Imogen. "I wonder where they keep the choir music?"

Half an hour later, Septimus returned.

"So sorry. That took longer than I anticipated."

"Do you think Harriet really wanted to talk about the Harvest Festival order of service?" asked Ophelia.

Septimus reared back his head. "You can't seriously think…?" He stopped and his nose quivered. "I suppose, as you pointed out, I must suspect everyone."

"That is the downside to fighting crime. You may have to suspect your friends, at least, initially."

"Harriet *is* in charge of printing the order of service for high days and holidays," he said thoughtfully. "But it was odd for her to come down to the crypt. If she was coming to the treasury and saw me, it might have just been a convenient excuse to explain her presence."

"Our minds have been traveling similar paths, Verger. We were wondering if this cache of treasure is widely known?"

Septimus's lips did a jig. "No! We keep a very low profile concerning this vault. Only the former vicar, Reverend Cresswell, and I know the extent of the wealth hidden here. I am very careful not to enter when I know others are in the church building. This vault is not what one might call a secure facility, so our best defense is ignorance of the fortune's existence."

"But the thief has discovered it," Imogen pointed out.

The verger's face fell. "Yes."

"It might be time to upgrade your level of protection," said Ophelia.

"Having never had a problem, I suppose the church has been lax in its security measures. I shall bring it up to Bartholomew at our next meeting. I won't mention the thefts of course, but I can introduce the notion of improving the lock."

"You've lived in Saffron Weald a long time," continued Ophelia. "Have you heard any rumors about the butcher having financial difficulties?"

His face creased in thought. "On the contrary. I believe they just completed some extensive redecorating in their flat above the shop."

Imogen had an idea. "Have you been surprised by any other unexpected visitors in the crypt recently?"

Septimus pondered the question. "Only those who should be here, like the choir director since the music is in a closet, the flower ladies whose supplies are in one of the cupboards, the deacon…oh, and the altar boys."

"Well, if you discover anyone who shouldn't be down here, be sure to let us know."

They bid him farewell.

"I fancy some lamb chops for dinner," said Imogen with a wink as they emerged into the sunny churchyard. "What about you?"

"Splendid idea! Strike while the iron is hot. I just hope Harold is not too punny today. It's like nails on a blackboard to me."

"Oh, don't be such a stick in the mud!" responded Imogen. "I think his jokes are lovely."

Ophelia grumbled something incoherent.

If Dickens had ever created a butcher, he might have used Harold Cleaver for his model. Though the style was terribly outdated, he wore mutton chop whiskers and a straw boater with a black band. The burly man welcomed them with a broad smile, his sign, *"Cleaver's. Where quality 'meats' affordability"* in the background. Imogen grinned at a new sign on the counter. *"Our sausages are the 'wurst'...in the best possible way."*

"Ladies! My, how you've brightened my day. I've just received a delivery of *amoozing* beef, haha. Want to *steak* a claim?"

While Ophelia was busy groaning, Imogen thanked him for the tip but explained that they were in the mood for lamb.

"*Lamb-tastic* choice! My chops are *shear* perfection." He made a scissor action with his fingers.

Imogen leaned into her dainty laughter in hopes that Harold would not notice Ophelia rolling her eyes.

"Perfect! We'll take two."

"Did I hear you've done some renovations upstairs," said Ophelia to get the ball rolling in the right direction. "I remember the flat from when I was young."

"You heard right!" he beamed. "We've had a good year and Harriet wanted to brighten the place up a bit. Got beautiful rose wallpaper in the sitting room now."

He pulled out the tray of chops and placed two on his scales. He gave Ophelia the side-eye. "Speaking of our youth, Jeffrey is coming for a visit next week. Did you know he's a widower?"

A look of alarm shone from Ophelia's face. "Is that so?"

"Perhaps we'll invite you two young ladies over for supper while he's here and you can see our improvements for yourselves."

Ophelia glared at her sister, hoping she was sufficiently communicating her distaste for the idea.

"Oh, um, that's very kind of you, Harold. I'll have to check our calendar." Imogen had no idea why her sister was so opposed to the idea. The thought of reminiscing with childhood friends was very appealing to her. "So, you enjoyed a profitable year? How nice."

"Oh, yes. The current market has been very good for us. The meat industry is finally bouncing back from the war years. The price of beef went down which means our sales went up. We're even considering a holiday to Cornwall, if I can get Harriet to agree. I feel like we deserve it."

"Lovely!" exclaimed Imogen as the cat seemed to have attacked Ophelia's tongue. "*We* used to holiday in Devon. Such a picturesque area of the country."

"That it is." He handed her the neatly wrapped package of chops. "How's that dog of yours? Tiny, isn't it?"

"We renamed him," Ophelia retorted. "His old name was such a misnomer. He's called Tiger now."

Harold chuckled. "Much more appropriate. If I needed to *beef* up security, I might be tempted to get a guard dog, but there's no need in a sleepy place like Saffron Weald and we live upstairs. Not the best for a dog."

"May I remind you that we had a quadruple killer living in our midst," growled Ophelia, whose high color indicated that she was close to the edge of losing her temper.

It was time to leave.

Thankfully, not even Ophelia's rudeness could dampen the friendly man's good humor. He whistled. "That's true. I still can't believe it. Connie, of all people. Who would've thought?" He shook his head in disbelief as Imogen handed him the money and hustled her sister out onto the pavement.

"*Hot crumpets!* What was all that about?" she demanded.

Ophelia's chest expanded, straining the buttons on her dress. "It's more than just his quirky humor," she began. "I didn't really ever tell you why Jeffrey and I broke it off all those years ago."

Imogen was all ears.

It was true. Her sister had remained uncharacteristically private about the whole affair back in 1883. But Imogen had been all wrapped up in her own romance and impending marriage and had not made the necessary time for her sister to indulge in a cathartic heart to heart. Then, by seemingly mutual, silent agreement, the sad topic had been buried, never to be spoken of again. Imogen still felt bad about her failure to be there for her sister in her time of need.

Was Ophelia ready to talk about it now?

Imogen threaded her arm through her sister's, and they slowly began to make their way home.

"Did you know the Cleavers come from a long line of punsters?" began Ophelia, looking straight ahead. "It actually only slightly annoyed me back in those days and I would just pretend to find their puns funny."

"Surely, you didn't break up with Jeffrey over his sense of humor," said Imogen gently.

"No! It was a whole mass of small things. I was blind to them initially, but they eventually made up one large mountain that helped me see we were not really suited to be life partners."

"Such as..." Imogen prodded.

"For a start he didn't like the opera. And before you say that's a silly reason, he didn't just dislike it, he absolutely hated it. And he wasn't really a fan of any classical music. He preferred music hall. Classical music was my life! Would he expect me not to play if we married? I would rather die.

"At first, I was just a lovesick fool because he was such a handsome, rugged fellow and had chosen me. But I was wearing rose-colored glasses. As time went on, it became increasingly obvious that he was less refined in his tastes than me. He enjoyed pig racing and romping around the countryside, while I enjoyed listening to brass bands in the park and memorizing Shakespeare's sonnets." Crossing the stone bridge over the pond, she continued. "I would gush about my longing to travel the whole world and Jeffrey would remark that he couldn't understand why anyone would ever want to leave England. Don't you see? He was so narrow in his view of the world and the future.

"One day, it all came to a head. He was suffocating me. But he was already planning the wedding. I felt trapped."

With Badger's Hollow now in view, Ophelia said, "I talked to Mother about my fears. She took me onto her lap like she had when we were children and soothed my aching soul. She assured me there would be other opportunities and that I should never be forced into a life that would constrict my talents, however handsome the package. She explained that she and Father were opposites who complemented each other and respected each other's differences. I could see that Jeffrey would expect me to conform to his ideas.

"I decided to break it off that night. Mother said she would arrange for me to travel up to the lake district to stay with Aunty Ivy and make a clean break."

Her recital of events stirred age old memories in Imogen. "I remember Mother telling me you were leaving for a while. I was confused. I was worried you wouldn't be back in time for your bridesmaid dress fitting." She grabbed her sister's arm as they stood at the gate. "I was so self-centered. Can you forgive me?"

Ophelia turned to hug her. "There's nothing to forgive, ducky. Of course you were all about your big day—that's as it should be. I didn't want my drama to overshadow your happiness. So, I left while you were away to get my head together."

"How did Jeffrey take it?"

"Not well. Not well at all. He thought he was the cat's whiskers and in truth, in our village, he was. He couldn't believe I was rejecting him. That's why he didn't become a butcher with his father. He couldn't take the embarrassment of it all. Almost immediately, he moved—to Colchester, I think. It was very messy. I struggled to keep up appearances for your wedding and then I fell apart. Mother was so good to me. That's when I said I wanted to move to London. Mother and Father agreed. Fresh start."

Fragments of images shifted position in Imogen's brain making a more complete, albeit fragmented, picture. "I still should have asked you about it," she murmured.

"You did! Don't you remember? I shut you down. It was too painful. I asked Mother not to mention it ever again either."

The ache of regret in Imogen's chest eased.

They wandered up the garden path and before putting the key in the lock she grabbed her sister's hands. "We can make up some excuse for not going to dinner." She grinned then gave a little cough. "In fact, I think I see a bout of the flu coming on."

Chapter 6

Once inside, Ophelia went straight to her violin and began to play an extremely mournful tune. Imogen gave her space and took Tiger out into the garden. It was a changeable day with puffy clouds racing along hiding the sun every five seconds.

She headed for the reading bench under the willow. It had still not been repainted and the flakes of white paint lay underneath like dandruff. She brushed the seat with her fingers to remove the most obvious paint chips then sat with a book she had pulled from the bookshelf; *North and South* by Elizabeth Gaskell. The leather-bound tome was worn at the corners, the spine cracked like the face of an old man. As a girl it had been one of her favorites.

Sensing this was not the time for play, Tiger curled up by her feet as she leaned against the willow's trunk.

As she read of Margaret Hale's clergyman father, she reflected on their morning with the verger, Septimus Saville. If not for his assiduous attention to detail, the theft would never have been discovered. She thought about the clues they had found; the lighter, the drop of wax and the cassock. Taken individually, they did not mean much, but as their investigation progressed, she hoped at least one of them would point to the thief.

Ruff!

Imogen started. She had fallen asleep in the warmth of the late summer afternoon. Blinking several times to clear the sleep from her eyes, she stretched her arms as Ophelia pushed through the back door with a man. Imogen shielded her eyes.

"We have a visitor," announced Ophelia as Tiger started sniffing the man's shoes with a slight grumble in the back of his throat.

"Deacon Purchase. What a lovely surprise." Simon Purchase was to plump what Septimus was to thin. A smile appeared on his round face but it did not reach his small eyes.

"How are the children?" Imogen continued moving over and motioning to the deacon that he should take the other half of the seat. She pulled Tiger beside her. "Shall we get some tea?"

"Not for me, thank you," said Simon, wiping his broad brow with a handkerchief. "I have just had some with Mrs. Tumblethorn."

"Then what can we do for you?" asked Ophelia, coming to stand in the shade of the tree.

His head swung around on his shoulders. "It's a rather delicate matter," he said, quietly.

Wondering how Simon knew, since Septimus claimed to have kept the matter of the theft to himself, Ophelia was about to assure him that things were in hand when he pre-empted her.

"Someone is stealing church funds."

A quick glance passed between the twins.

"I'm in charge of monies; Sunday collections, fundraising efforts, the Sunday School outing fund and the choir finances," he continued, wiping his lips with the back of his hand. "I take funds collected during Sunday worship and make an accounting of all that is donated immediately. I also check the collection boxes for the Sunday School and choir but only collect that money quarterly. On Mondays, I take most of the money from the collection plates to the bank, keeping a little on hand for necessities."

"Is the money kept in a safe before heading to the bank?" asked Imogen, thinking of the one her husband had used.

He wiggled his fingers. "Uh-no. We have a petty cash box that we keep in a cupboard in the vicar's office. But it's not that money that is missing. It's the collection box funds." He scratched his head and took a deep breath. "I check them by weight until I empty them on the quarter. The first couple of times, I thought I was imagining it since it's not a very exact method, but now it has happened four times. The boxes are getting lighter and lighter."

"Have you told the police?" asked Ophelia.

A sharp line formed between his dark eyebrows. "No! I want to keep it all hush hush and put a stop to it without making a big todo."

Tiger stirred in reaction to the deacon's animation and Imogen soothed him. "What does the vicar say?"

The line deepened. "I haven't told the vicar. He wouldn't suspect me or anything but he would have to report it to his superiors…and they aren't as understanding. I'm sure I would be dismissed and my wife and I depend on the stipend. My woodworking business doesn't quite make ends meet and what with the new baby..." He shifted on the bench and several more flakes of paint fluttered their way to the grass. "Besides, it will dent my reputation. You two seem to have a knack for detecting, so I thought I'd come to you first."

Cap now clutched between his hands, his eyes darted from twin to twin.

Ophelia sat down on the arm of the bench next to her sister. "Can you tell us about these permanent collection boxes?"

"Those are secured wooden boxes in locations around the church. I count the money at the end of the quarter and report to the church how close we are to certain financial goals. But for those three months the money remains in the box."

"And how do you access the boxes?"

"With a small key. I slide the box out and there's a little door in the back. From time to time, I detach the boxes from the wall to feel the weight and see how we are doing. Last week when I checked, the Sunday School trip fund was significantly lighter than the month before." He raised anxious eyes. "I don't want to make a fuss. I just want to discreetly find out who it is and ask them to stop or see if they need financial help. I won't prosecute or anything. But if this keeps going on, I'll be blamed for it as sure as apples is apples."

Ophelia clasped her hands. "My conclusion is that absolutely anyone could gain access to the funds by jimmying the fundraising boxes."

The glint of hope that had managed to fight its way onto his features fell off. "That's about the shape of it. Yes. Can you help?"

"We're not trained investigators, of course, but we can certainly undertake some surveillance," replied Ophelia.

"*Surveillance?*" thought Imogen. "How on earth does a term like that slip off Ophelia's tongue?

"I'd be ever so grateful. A big fellow like me hiding round corners would be more than obvious. I really appreciate it."

He hefted his large frame up and placed the cap on his head. Tiger lifted his snout with mild interest.

"Do you think it's the same thief?" asked Imogen as she watched the deacon leave their garden.

"I don't know what to think," murmured Ophelia. "But it seems a reasonable assumption."

"What happened to the idyllic village of our childhood?" asked Imogen, rubbing Tiger behind the ears. "Or were we just blissfully ignorant?"

Ophelia wrung her hands. "It certainly seems as though the Great War unleashed an evil that can't be put back in the bottle."

Chapter 7

*T*umblethorn's, Saffron Weald's grocer, was housed in the same Elizabethan style building as the rest of the village. It had been a grocer's shop for three generations. The eccentric Reginald Tumblethorn ran the store while taking care of his invalid mother.

"Imogen! Ophelia! What a pleasure to see you." He adjusted the cuffs of his blousy Regency shirt then touched the knot at the neck.

The whole store was arranged alphabetically, with a new, eclectic item for sale each week that Reggie picked up from…somewhere.

"Good morning, Reggie!" returned Ophelia. "What's the special today?"

Adopting the expression of a mouse on the hunt for cheese, his nose wrinkled and he leaned forward as if spilling national security secrets. "I picked up some pickled watermelon yesterday from America. They'll fly off the shelves as soon as word is out so I'm telling people individually to avoid a rush."

Ophelia kept her eyes on Reggie for fear that if she looked at her sister, they would burst into uncontrollable laughter. "Pickled watermelon. H-how exotic." She put a hand to her mouth.

"Shall I put some aside for you?" The innocence in his hopefulness was heart melting.

"Let's see, shall we?" said Imogen vaguely.

"Don't wait too long," he warned. "I'll be in the back with mother. Holler when you're ready."

"I didn't think we could ask him about the choir stuff while I was trying to hold in a guffaw," explained Ophelia.

"Totally agree. Where *does* he find these things?"

They pottered about, picking up bits and pieces then reassembled at the counter and slapped the bell.

Reggie pushed through the beaded curtain. "Ready?"

"How long have you been in the choir, Reggie?" asked Imogen.

He stopped picking up their items and looked into the distance. "Hmm. About six years. How did you like it?"

"Marvelous. Douglas is a real pro. I appreciate that," responded Ophelia.

"I'm sure you do," he replied getting back to sorting the items. "His attention to detail is what makes our choir stand out."

"Does everyone get along?" asked Imogen.

Reggie tipped his head and a brow followed suit. "Well, you didn't hear it from me, but Agatha and Patricia have a longstanding rivalry—family stuff dating way back."

"We know! Heard them going at it hammer and tongs as we left the church," said Ophelia.

"You'd think that two intelligent women would be able to bury the hatchet but the animosity is still rather intense."

"Any others with an axe to grind?" Ophelia asked.

"Desmond and the colonel don't always see eye to eye but they keep it professional most of the time."

Ophelia considered this statement. Desmond was a 'hail-fellow-well-met' personality, whereas the colonel was extremely rigid.

"How are things at the *Dog and Whistle*?" asked Ophelia. "We've only been in there once since our return. Looks like business is booming."

"Oh, it is. Never better. I like to go in for a game of darts now and again. Des is such a friendly soul. Makes it feel like a real home from home."

"And what about you? Is trade good?" asked Imogen.

Reggie drew continuous circles in the air in front of him as if he were about to take off. "These specials bring people in droves. Do you know, they come in even if they don't need anything just to see what the special is. Mother says I have a keen head for business." He added up the total. "Shall I add a bottle of the pickled watermelon?"

Imogen responded while Ophelia choked on a snicker. "We wouldn't want to take any from another customer."

He ran a hand down the front of his shirt. "Very well. But several have gone already; Gladys, Agatha, Desmond. Don't say I didn't warn you!"

Out on the pavement, they bumped into Agatha Trumble, the headmistress of the primary school. Literally. She rocked on her heels as Imogen reached out to steady her.

"Oh, excuse us!" cried Ophelia.

"Think nothing of it. I meant to catch you after choir. Did you enjoy it?" She adjusted a rather battered straw hat.

"Very enjoyable. Douglas certainly knows how to draw the best out of us," responded Imogen.

Agatha put her gloved hands together as if in prayer and looked heavenward. "That man is a genius." Her gloves were worn and bore a little hole in one of the fingers.

"How long have *you* been with the choir?" asked Ophelia.

"Goodness! Let me see. It was shortly after I began teaching. Must be twenty years." Her palm went to her chest. "How time flies."

"And are you enjoying your summer off?"

"Oh, yes! Of course, I love the children but it *is* nice to re-energize over the summer. And I've managed to cultivate a bumper crop in my vegetable garden this year." Her expression became strained. "Just as well since my thatched roof needs re-doing. Every time it rains, the roof leaks. Don't know where I'm going to find the money from."

"I'm sorry to hear that," lamented Imogen. "It is such an expense."

"And all on the tail of having my leaded windows mended last year. I love old houses but if it's not one thing, it's another. Now, if you'll excuse me." She pushed into *Tumblethorn's*.

Ophelia's face radiated excitement. "That's one choir member in need of money. Now, shall we go home and see what damage Tiger has done?"

"I was thinking, since we're in town, we could go to the teashop. We visit them in every other place we travel but have yet to stop by the one in our own village. That way we can talk to Matilda."

"Alright. But we shouldn't be long."

The tea shop was located at the other end of the high street, A little flag posted outside proclaimed its wares with a skillfully drawn dainty cake next to a floral teacup. *Thyme for Tea* was utterly feminine, from the tables for two, painted a faint pink, to the large, hand crocheted doilies that graced each tabletop instead of cloths, to the watercolors of the English countryside that covered the walls and the fussy, lace curtains at the windows.

Several people raised a hand in acknowledgement as they entered; Harriet Cleaver with Alice Puddingfield, and Prudence Cresswell with Mildred Chumbley. The tightness of the skin across Prudence's jaw betrayed the state of their interaction.

"Welcome!" trilled Matilda brightly. "It's lovely to see you here. Since this is your inaugural visit, the first pot is on the house."

"How very kind," said Imogen, wondering if this was a back-handed criticism.

"I have a lovely seat by the window."

Once they were settled and had ordered, Ophelia looked out the window. "Look!"

She directed Imogen to a spot on the other side of the street where Agatha and Patricia, the postmistress and distant cousin, were at it again. It was not necessary to hear the words to know that their conversation had reached boiling point.

"I wonder if Agatha is daring to ask for money to repair her cottage," mused Imogen.

"Quite possibly. She may feel entitled to some of the old money. I should like to find out the details of the feud."

Matilda Butterworth returned, laden with goodies. Ophelia recognized one of Alice's new biscuits.

"It's so lovely when old families return to the village," Matilda said as she placed the tray on the table.

"Can you sit for a minute?" asked Ophelia.

Matilda looked around then pulled up a chair from another table. "Since it's quiet right now I don't see any problem in that." She picked up one of the delicious biscuits. "How is the cottage? Did it need any refreshing?"

"As a matter of fact, it did." The sisters recited all the changes they had made to a dwelling that still carried the strong signature of their mother and father.

"I must tell you that I'm still in shock about Connie," Matilda gasped when they had finished. "How do you live around someone for years and not know they are a stone-cold killer?"

"I suppose if guilt were written on our foreheads, it would remove the need for a police force and justice system," chuckled Imogen.

"I think the thing that bothers me the most is that she obviously felt so little remorse," declared Matilda. "Then she had the audacity to put on the charade of being so scared she had to get a dog."

"Not only that, she came over bold as brass to welcome us home and bring me a book, knowing full well she had murdered our mother," pointed out Imogen.

Matilda tutted. "We don't really know each other at all, do we?"

They all tsked in triplicate.

"It appears your little venture is doing well," remarked Ophelia, looking around.

"Can't complain," responded Matilda. "I even have some savings put away to take a nice trip to the coast in September."

"That's marvelous," said Imogen.

"How long have you played the organ for the choir?" asked Ophelia.

"Donkey's years. I began piano lessons at a very young age then my mother insisted I learn how to play the organ. I started playing for church services when I was only fourteen."

"You're very good. Do you enjoy it?"

"Douglas can be a bit of a tartar at times, but on the whole, I do. It gets me out of the house and I like the people in the choir. I consider them my friends. You have to be careful not to hide yourself away when you're single. Don't you agree, Ophelia?"

"Indeed! I was hardly ever home."

The bell on the door rang and another customer entered. "Nice talking to you, but duty calls."

"So far, only Agatha is hurting for money," whispered Ophelia. "Like we told Septimus and Simon, we need to conduct surveillance to catch the culprit in the act."

Chapter 8

Thursday evening, the twins made sure to eat dinner early. Imogen was surprised to find that she was quite looking forward to choir practice. As they collected their hats and handbags, Tiger watched them with sad eyes.

"I'll throw a ball in the garden for you when we get back, lovey," promised Imogen, holding his head behind the ears and nestling her nose into his fur.

"Hurry up, ducky," said Ophelia. "I want to watch people arrive to see how they interact with each other before choir practice begins. And don't forget we're hiding out in the crypt afterward, so you might not be able to keep your promise to Tiger."

"Oh, yes." She kissed the dog. "Well, for sure tomorrow then."

The church was only a five-minute walk from their house and Ophelia was glad to see they were the first arrivals. Instead of sitting in the choir stall, they opted to sit on the first row of pews.

Reggie arrived next. Today he wore scarlet trousers with a green shirt, purple braces and a jaunty hat.

"Ladies! So good to see you again." He came to sit near them on the pew.

"How's the sale of pickled watermelon?" asked Ophelia with a rigidly straight face.

Reggie reached an arm along the pew. "Steady and sure. You should snap one up before they're gone."

The arrival of the colonel interrupted further dissection of the watermelon sales. He wore a light linen suit and Panama hat. Despite his advanced age, he was ramrod straight, walking without the aid of a cane.

He dipped his head in greeting as he removed his hat. "Imogen. Ophelia. Douglas not here yet?"

"We haven't seen him. Have a seat while you wait." Imogen remembered how uncomfortable her feet had felt after an hour of standing.

"Don't mind if I do." He sat down and stretched out his long legs.

Clip, clop.

Ophelia looked up to see Agatha mincing her way down the aisle in unexpected heels and dressed as though it were Sunday rather than Thursday. Her understated eyes scanned the empty pews as if searching for someone.

"No Douglas?" she asked. "I've never known him to be late before."

"Me neither," said the colonel.

Desmond Ale, proprietor of the pub, entered next, his jolly, mustached face ruddy with goodwill. "Cheers!"

The colonel grumbled.

Prudence Cresswell and Arabella Fudgeford arrived together in friendly conversation about their children. They chattered all the way to the front of the church until they realized that no one was in the choir stalls.

"Where's Douglas? I think we should get ready. He must be delayed," declared Prudence.

Matilda, the organist, arrived with haste in her step. "Sorry I'm late, Douglas—" She stopped. "Oh, he's not here yet either. Just as well for me." She hurried up the steps to the organ.

Celina, Harriet and Patricia arrived together and stopped, viewing the clustered group.

"What's up?" asked Celina.

"We don't know," replied Reggie. "Douglas seems to have been held up."

"Well, that's a first," she replied.

Algernon Wainright, local historian, lumbered through the doorway with his cane. Considering he was in his late eighties, he was relatively spry.

"I think we should get into our positions," he admonished.

"That's what I said," declared Prudence, her eyes roving the room.

"Matilda, can you run us through some scales?" continued Algernon. "Shows some initiative."

The choir members dispersed to their positions in the choir stalls where they found their music on the seats as Archie ran up the center of the church, puffing. "Sorry! I had a late delivery of flour to see to."

The distinctive sound of organ music filled the church.

"I can lead until he arrives," offered Ophelia, moving to the director's position and placing her music on the wooden stand.

Once their voices were warmed up and Douglas still had not appeared, Ophelia began leading them in the song for the Harvest Festival.

With the ease of the professional she was, she led them easily through the difficult parts and after singing it once, reviewed some of the harmony with the basses and altos.

Imogen couldn't help but smile. Music was Ophelia's milieu and she was never happier than when immersed in it. Closing her eyes, her sister swayed as she led the choir through the music a second time.

After the third time through, Ophelia directed the choir to take out the piece they had not practiced the week before. Even though it was a song Imogen had never encountered, Ophelia had played it on the piano at home through the week to ensure that Imogen felt comfortable with the new number.

Ophelia led them through the parts and was tapping the music stand to run through it all together when a strangled cry stopped everyone.

"Ahhh!"

"What the dickens was that?" barked the colonel. The sound had come from behind the altar and they all turned their heads as one.

Before their eyes, a hunched figure staggered from behind the curtain, eyes locked on their hands.

Hands that were covered in crimson blood.

Douglas looked up, eyes bulging with agitation and terror.

"S-Septimus. He's d-dead."

Chapter 9

"Ahhhh!"

Ear splitting shards of anguish slashed the still air of the church, pouring from Agatha's mouth like a raging waterfall. The dreadful, double-sided blades of sound stabbed the hearts of everyone within range, the famed acoustics of the church intensifying the awful wailing.

Imogen squeezed her eyes shut in pain.

Douglas slumped into a pew unsure where to put his bloodied hands.

"Where is he?" demanded Ophelia, taking charge and rushing to Douglas's side as Agatha continued her hysterical shrieking.

"I-i-in the crypt. I went down to get some m-m-music." His face drained and Ophelia feared he was going to buckle under the horror of what he had witnessed.

"Agatha! Shut up! Harriet, come down here for Douglas."

The colonel grabbed Agatha's arms and shook her, but nothing helped.

A stunned Harriet went to the fainting man as the rest of the choir members buzzed with frantic fear amid the caterwauling.

"Imogen!"

Gathering her wits about her, Imogen joined her sister.

"Let's go!"

Shoes crunching on the stone floor, the sisters each took a deep breath before heading down into the crypt. A murky twilight penetrated the gloom through high, slit windows as they made their careful way through the coffins of the noble dead.

"Oh!" cried Imogen. "So much blood!"

Slouched against the wall, just outside the open vault door, lay Septimus, a large, bedazzled dagger sticking from his back.

"Poor Septimus," she groaned.

"We shouldn't really move anything," murmured Ophelia, dropping into a crouch by the body. "But I think it prudent to look around before the police arrive." She blew out a couple of deep breaths before feeling for a pulse then reaching into the dead man's jacket.

Plucking a sheet of paper from his inside pocket she read, "A memorandum. *Check the candles.*" Ophelia looked up. "That must be since our last visit with him down here."

Glancing into the open vault, Imogen said, "I'll make an educated guess that the dagger is one of the church's treasures which, given our previous knowledge, would lead me to surmise that the verger surprised someone in the act of stealing something. I don't think it's a leap to suggest that the thief panicked, grabbed the knife and plunged it into Septimus's back."

"I agree that is the most likely theory." Ophelia was delving into the other side of the jacket and both outside pockets. She withdrew a package of breath mints and the key to the vault. "However, we should keep an open mind. We need to consider that this may have nothing to do with the thefts." She tipped her head. "Can you smell that?"

"All I can smell is mustiness and mold," replied Imogen, looking everywhere but at the unfortunate verger's waxy face.

Ophelia leaned closer to the body. "Vinegar." She picked up one of the verger's hands and sniffed his fingers. Then she moved to his arm. "Vinegar, but only on the sleeve. Strange."

"It *is* after dinner. Perhaps he had something pickled with his meal."

Ophelia's brow wiggled. "Could be. I moved his arm easily. He hasn't been dead for more than a few hours."

"That means he was killed not long before choir practice began," responded Imogen.

"I'd be surprised if it was one of the choir members," said Ophelia. "They'd have to be a pretty hardened individual to strike out in a panic, killing a man down here then leaving him to bleed to death, all the while arriving for practice as if nothing was wrong."

Imogen lifted her palms. "If appearing innocent was the only way to save you from the noose, you'd make a good shot at it too."

"Point taken." Ophelia shifted, still crouched. "Here's a piece of blue thread on his jacket. Quick, put it in your handbag."

"Is that proper? Shouldn't we leave everything just as we find it?"

"Oh, alright. If you must be a stickler for protocol." Ophelia shifted to the left. "Too bad I don't have Septimus's torch. It's really difficult to see anything clearly down here."

As Imogen took a step forward, she noticed something glinting. Bending over, she found a tiny jewel, the kind that would make up a brooch. Holding it up to the dim light, she recognized it as amber. "Look!"

"Well done, ducky!"

"I shall put it back where it was for the police to find. It may have dropped from the dagger."

The knife was jammed against the stone wall as if Septimus had staggered backward. "I can't tell without moving him and moving a corpse before the officials arrive is definitely prohibited."

Ophelia's knees creaked as she stood. "I'm glad we've been able to assess the scene before the police get here. Unfortunately, there's nothing else we can do for the poor man. We should go back upstairs."

"Septimus Saville is indeed dead," announced Ophelia as they re-entered the sanctuary.

A chorus of 'ohs' sounded.

Douglas had revived a little but this news drained his color again. A silent but trembling Agatha was now on the pew beside him clutching her heart.

"Someone needs to go for Constable Hargrove," she continued.

"I've already sent Celina," said the colonel.

"Thank you."

Imogen took stock of the remaining choir members. Harriet was still fanning the choir director. Prudence Cresswell and Arabella Fudgeford were comforting each other while Patricia

Snodgrass and Matilda Butterworth sat in rigid silence. As for the men, Reggie looked a bit green around the gills and had a clammy hand to his mouth. Algernon sat lips open, veined hand resting on his cane, and Archie was shaking his head in stunned disbelief. Meanwhile, the colonel's nails drummed the wooden handrail of the choir stalls, and Simon, the deacon, was running frantic fingers through his thinning hair. Only Desmond seemed animated, though the hard lines on his features betrayed his state of mind.

"I'd like to pop home and bring back some brandy," he suddenly suggested. "We'll all have to stay until Hargrove has arrived and questioned us. I think a shot of the stuff will help everyone cope."

"Splendid idea," agreed Ophelia. "As long as you hurry right back."

Des slipped down the few stairs of the choir stalls on stubby legs, ran down the aisle rocking from side to side, and fled out the door. For a fleeting moment, Ophelia thought he might be the murderer making his escape.

Imogen sat beside Douglas. "Can you tell me exactly what happened, lovey?

He held a bloodied handkerchief in shaky hands. "I-I arrived about ten minutes early as I wanted to check on some old choir music. We k-keep it in the cupboard in the crypt. I was thinking of adding a choir number to the s-service. It's dark down there and I didn't have a t-torch, but I hoped the light from those small windows would be s-sufficient. Before I reached the cabinet that houses the music, I-I tripped over something. When I looked, I saw it was shoes. I remember thinking it was strange. Then my eyes traveled up and I saw S..." A sob escaped. "It was Septimus. Dead eyed. His legs jutting out into the passage. B-blood was just oozing out of him." He raised haunted eyes. "I must have passed out as everything went black." He reached up a blood-stained hand to touch the back of his head.

Ophelia parted his hair and found a large, purple goose egg. He winced as she touched it.

"Ow!"

"You'll need to get that seen to," she said.

He pulled on the handkerchief. "When I came to, I was s-still woozy. I thought I should check to see if he was d-dead or if I needed to call a doctor so I-I felt for a pulse and took hold of the dagger to pull it out, then thought better of it. But there was blood all over my hands and I-I felt faint again. I could hear you all singing so I struggled against the nausea to climb the stairs to get help."

Desmond was back with a bottle of brandy and a tray of small glasses. "You look like you need it the most, mate," he said, pouring a snifter for Douglas who knocked it back like a thirsty man in the desert.

As Des served the other choir members, Celina returned with Constable Hargrove in tow. Hargrove was middle-aged and a pro at finding cats and settling arguments. Murder was out of his league and his shoulders and jaw were stiff as a board.

"Everyone stay here," he blustered. "I'm going to take a look at the body."

"Would you like us to accompany you?" asked Imogen, since they had been present at the last murder.

An emotion that resembled relief flooded his anxious features.

"Since you asked, Mrs. Pettigrew, I think I would."

"Then follow us," said Ophelia leading the way. "Do you carry a torch, Constable?"

He patted his side. "Always."

"Then I suggest you get it out. It's rather dreary in the crypt."

They crunched their way down the steps and the constable ducked his head at the bottom. Imogen led the way to the dead body.

"Oh!" cried out the policeman and slammed a handkerchief to his lips.

"It never gets easier, does it, Constable?" soothed Ophelia, giving the policeman a moment to regain his composure. One could almost see his stomach roll beneath his uniform.

Guiding him to the body, they pointed out the things they had already noticed but the rapid movement of his eyes led to the conclusion that he was not taking much of it in.

"Shouldn't you be writing all this down?" asked Imogen. "For the inspector?"

The constable reached for his notebook and pencil with trembling fingers and began to write in an extremely wobbly hand.

Once they had gone through everything they had noticed previously, Ophelia confessed, "I think we should tell you that Septimus had approached us professionally, Constable. Someone has been stealing treasures from the church vault." She indicated the open door. "He wanted to be discreet—didn't want to make a fuss, but worried he would be accused of the theft and lose his job."

Bloodshot eyes flicked to Ophelia's face. "What kinds of things?"

"Silver communion plates that were no longer in use. Some candlesticks. It was only because Septimus was such a good curator that he even noticed anything was missing." She pointed toward the open vault. "There's a huge pile of treasure beyond this door."

Hargrove coughed, avoiding the body with his gaze. "Is that so? I should check to see if anything else is missing."

A noise on the stairs caught their attention. Ophelia stepped out to stop the person, as the vicar appeared looking blanched and harried.

"I heard that Septimus has been murdered," he gasped.

"I'm afraid so," said Ophelia.

The vicar followed her then seeing the verger slumped against the wall, he covered his face with his hands. "Oh, no! He was my friend."

"Then I am doubly sorry," responded Ophelia, deciding how much to disclose. After all, Septimus had been their client.

"I think you should look in his pockets," she suggested to Constable Hargrove.

Abject horror crossed the policeman's face. "Uh-no. I'll let the inspector from Parkford do that."

"Well, if you're sure…" She was not about to tell him she had already looked.

Noticing the vault door open, the vicar murmured, "Killed in the line of duty."

"It would appear that way, Reverend. I need to check for missing items," said the constable. "Perhaps you could help me?"

All four of them stepped into the treasury as the vicar reached for the light switch.

"Woah! It's like the bloomin' Crown Jewels down here," gasped the constable as the light sprung to life. "How would you know if anything was gone?"

"Septimus kept scrupulous records," explained Reverend Cresswell. "To be honest, I had such complete faith in his organizational skills that I never really came down here. He should have his ledger on him. We can check things in here against his records."

The twins locked eyes. *Ledger?*

A noise behind them caused Ophelia to step out of the vault as Matilda Butterworth appeared.

"It's Agatha. She can't breathe. I think we need a doctor."

Chapter 10

Saffron Weald did not have its own doctor. The closest was the one in Parkford, the county seat. Constable Hargrove gave permission for the doctor to be called and asked the vicar to stay with the body while he went upstairs to question the choir members while they awaited the arrival of Inspector Southam. The twins followed.

Matilda had not exaggerated. Agatha was in bad shape, grasping her chest, needles of pain shooting down her face. Thankfully, the colonel was in charge, holding her hand while encouraging her to regulate her breathing. Ophelia hoped they wouldn't have another death on their hands.

Imogen grabbed the handbag she had forgotten in her haste. "Prudence, I need to use your telephone."

The vicar's wife stirred as if the words hadn't quite registered.

"Let's hurry!" encouraged Imogen.

The vicarage was not as old as the other homes of the village. An l-shaped structure, the front door was placed where the two angles met. A neatly trimmed thatch roof bowed down to meet the ivy-clad, whitish stone walls. The courtyard possessed a large, circular structure that held a raised flower garden, surrounded by a gravel drive. The whole was crowded by a large assembly of pine trees.

Prudence flew through the door, Imogen hot on her tail.

A young girl stood wide eyed, drinking from a glass, as the pair filled the hall with nervous energy.

Prudence pointed to the telephone. "Do you think I should go back?"

"Yes. I think Hargrove will want to talk to everyone before we go home," replied Imogen.

Prudence made for the door again.

"Where's Mummy going?" asked the girl, who could not be more than fourteen.

"Back to choir practice."

The girl's eyes narrowed as she peppered Imogen with questions. "And why do you need the telephone? Why does Constable Hargrove want to talk to Mummy. He isn't a member of the choir."

Sharp girl.

"Someone has been taken ill," explained Imogen. "I'm calling for the doctor."

They undertook a staring match as Imogen waited for the vicar's daughter to leave before using the instrument.

Task completed, Imogen hurried back.

A crowd of choir members now stood in a circle around Agatha who was panting and sweating profusely, her mottled skin a dangerous hue of white ash.

"The doctor is on his way," Imogen declared.

As for Douglas, he had a little more color in his face than when she left.

"I'm feeling rather jumpy," said Patricia Snodgrass, the usually sedate post mistress, as Imogen joined the circle. "I can't stop thinking about poor Septimus. That man wouldn't hurt a fly."

Imogen glanced up in time to see Harriet Cleaver snort a little bit of snuff.

A clatter of boots heralded the arrival of the constable.

"I have set up the vicar's office as an interview room. I shall need to get a start on everyone's statement before the inspector arrives," Hargrove declared.

If they were going to be stuck at the church for the foreseeable future, Ophelia was going to use the time profitably. She withdrew from the concerned circle surrounding Agatha and sat on the first pew next to Douglas.

"What a shock to find Septimus down there," she began, with an exaggerated sigh.

Douglas whimpered. "I have to admit the crypt is not one of my favorite places to begin with. Gives me the willies at the best of times and to find..." He took a moment to compose himself. "I've often spoken to Bartholomew about moving the music upstairs, but he claims there is no room."

"So, you were down there looking for more music?" she prompted when he stopped.

"Yes, we're singing for the opening and benediction hymns for the Harvest Festival and I thought it might be worthwhile to sing an intermediate hymn too. I had one in mind that we sang several years ago. It would take me no more than two minutes to find it." He rubbed his head where the goose egg protruded. "At first, I had no idea what I had fallen over. I thought perhaps someone had left something on the floor. I can't tell you what it did to me to see that I had tripped over a pair of feet. Then seeing his lifeless face and the blood…" He paused again and wiped his nose. "I dare say it's not very manly of me to faint, but it was all too much."

"Were you two friends?" Ophelia asked, watching Imogen as her sister scanned the faces of the rest of the group.

"Friends? I wouldn't say friends, no." He threaded his quivering, blood-stained fingers. "Acquaintances, yes. I'm over at the church every Thursday and Sunday and we bump into each other on occasion. He seems like a nice chap but we had little in common."

"Do you know if he had a particular friend, as they say?"

Douglas closed one eye and slid his jaw to the right. "I'm not sure. Bartholomew perhaps. I think he sometimes went bird watching with Reggie."

"Do you ever go into the crypt for anything else?" she prodded, eager to pump him for information while he was willing.

His eyes flashed to hers. "Why? I told you, I hate it down there."

"Of course." She cast around for something else to ask but came up blank. "When the doctor gets here, I'll have him take a look at your head."

"That would be marvelous," he groaned, wincing.

Patricia had moved out of the inner circle that had gathered around the ailing Agatha.

"We need to give her more air," she explained to Ophelia.

"I didn't know you two were related until recently," Ophelia commented.

A shadow of hatred passed over her no-nonsense features, evaporating quickly. "We are second cousins. But our families are not close."

"Oh?"

Patricia sat next to Ophelia on the bench and exhaled. "The long and the short of it is, over one hundred years ago, our common great-great-grandfather died suddenly of a heart attack while out on his pasture. He had not made a will. My great-grandfather was the oldest son and the magistrate awarded him the whole farm. But according to the other two brothers, their father had made it clear he wanted *all* his sons to inherit the farm by dividing it three ways. My great- grandfather refused saying there was no proof and that their claim was just hearsay. My great- great-grandmother pleaded with him to take care of his brothers but he refused as they had fallen out several years before.

"One of the brothers became so depressed about his future he killed himself, and the other, Agatha's great-grandfather, struggled to scrape a living by becoming a tinker. He died a poor man, with nothing to leave his own son, Agatha's grandfather. All this led to a feud between the two lines of the family that has never been breached."

Ophelia shrugged one shoulder. "Money does terrible things to families."

"Yes, but my grandfather, who inherited from my great-grandfather, worked very hard to try to make the farm profitable. Agatha's grandfather and then her father were always coming to my grandfather with their hands out until, frankly, it was embarrassing. Now, Agatha keeps coming to me demanding money for her roof. She insists that she is entitled to it because of our great-great-grandfather's wishes. What she doesn't understand is that over the generations, taxes and repairs dwindled the wealth as parcels of land were sold off to pay the bills. By the time my grandfather died, there was very little left to hand down to my father. Now that my parents are gone and since I never married, I have had to make my own way in the world. It's not like I have a pot of gold at the end of my bed."

Ophelia could appreciate the problem.

Her attention was caught by Reggie who was pushing Agatha into a sitting position. Her skin was beginning to pink up and Ophelia guessed that the emergency had passed.

Algernon returned from being questioned, leaning heavily on his cane. Unless he was acting, it was unlikely he could run up and down the stairs to kill Septimus and appear at the choir practice unruffled. He would be puffing and panting as if he had run a marathon. He held up his hat. "Forgot it with everything going on. Toodle-loo!"

The usually jolly Desmond left next to be questioned, pulling at his thick mustache.

"What do you know about Desmond?" Ophelia asked Patricia.

"Lovely man. He's a widower, now, as you know. Wife died unexpectedly over five years ago. The *Dog and Whistle* is a tied house, meaning that Desmond is not a local and was appointed to be the publican by the brewery that owns the pub. But he's been in Saffron Weald for the last twenty years and assimilated well." Patricia flicked her gloves. "His wife used to sing in the choir too. That's why he continues."

"And the brewery is happy with his performance?"

"Oh, yes. He got a bonus two years ago for significantly increasing profits."

"Did he?" So, he would be an unlikely thief. "Did he and his wife have any children?"

"A son. He died in the war. Very sad. I think it led to his wife's death, myself. It's surprising that Desmond can stay so cheerful, considering."

"Thank you for being so candid," said Ophelia, standing. "If you'll excuse me, I want to see how my sister is doing."

Patricia nodded. "Of course."

Wandering over to Imogen's side she whispered, "Found out anything interesting?"

Her sister's eyes flared. "Apparently, Agatha has a blood phobia, which is odd for a teacher. There must be plenty of scraped knees and bloody noses at school. And did you know that Celina and Arabella attend a dance class together in the next village? Not that it's relevant to the current situation but interesting, none the less. Archie is quite out of sorts. He and Septimus used to have a good natter when he came into the bakery. He's taken it badly. Just look at him."

Ophelia glanced over at her friend the baker. His active jaw betrayed his effort to hold back strong emotions.

"Prudence is already worrying about arrangements for the funeral as Septimus had no family," continued Imogen. "She doesn't want him having a pauper's funeral."

Ophelia shared what she had learned from Patricia and Douglas.

Constable Hargrove re-appeared. "Next."

The colonel stood. "If you don't mind, I'll go next. I have to be at a meeting soon."

Imogen glanced at her watch. It was now nine o'clock. Dusk was settling over the village. What meeting could he possibly have at this time of night?

Tiger!

Imogen had forgotten all about him. He would need to be let out soon or they would come home to an accident.

"I need to go next. I have to let the dog out," she told her sister.

Ophelia's brows popped. "*Flaming fiddles!* I'd forgotten about him, too. Let's hope he can hold it."

At that moment, Inspector Southam from Parkford, arrived. Ophelia and Imogen were well known to him, and he respected their wisdom after they helped catch the murderer who had struck at the village fête. He made a beeline for them.

"Why am I not surprised you two are here," he said with a wry grin.

Chapter 11

"We are bona fide members of the choir, Inspector." Imogen wiggled her choir music.

His dark eyes brightened as he swiped off his hat. "Is that right? Useful. Alright, give me a quick summary of what I'm dealing with here."

Once they had finished, he asked to be taken down to the crypt.

"Can I pop home and let the dog out, Inspector?" asked Imogen. "I'll be right back."

He flapped his hat at her. "Alright. But be quick about it."

It would only take her five minutes to see to Tiger and he could stay out until they returned home later that evening.

"Shall we?" The inspector gestured with his arm for Ophelia to go ahead of him.

"Watch your head," she said as they plunged down the ancient steps.

"Over here!" called the vicar.

Ophelia's chin dropped. Here was another thing she had forgotten. "Reverend Cresswell! You poor thing down here with Septimus all this time!"

"The constable asked me to stay, so that's what I did," he called out.

It was now positively inky in the crypt since night had fallen and Ophelia reached around for the light without success. "Where's the light switch, Vicar?"

"Near the bottom of the stairs."

Inspector Southam turned on his torch for Ophelia, illuminating the switch.

"This way," Ophelia directed.

They found the vicar next to the body that was still slumped against the wall, his long gangly legs outstretched. He struggled to his feet. "Inspector."

The dark puddle of blood had now congealed around the corpse.

"Vicar. Thank you for guarding the body. You can go now but I shall need to question you later."

Bartholomew Cresswell put a hand to his back and bent to the side. "Thank you."

Once he left, Inspector Southam moved deftly with the practiced movements of a professional. He soon found the memorandum about the candles.

"Uh, I should probably disclose that Septimus had come to Imogen and I, Inspector. Someone was stealing artifacts from the treasury."

He turned toward her in his crouched position. "What?"

"It's rather a long story but Septimus Saville is—was—a fastidious curator who kept detailed records of everything in the vault. When you see the extent of the church's treasures you will realize what a big job it was." Since the light was not inside the vault it appeared to be nothing more than a black hole. "He noticed that a couple of things had disappeared and asked us to look into it."

The inspector gestured to the body. "Do you think his death is connected to these suspicions?"

"Don't you?"

"It's far too early in the investigation for me to draw such a conclusion. And I don't know these people. I'm asking for your opinion."

"In that case, yes, I do. Septimus mentioned that the artifacts would disappear around choir practices."

The inspector swiveled back to the body. "Did *you* find anything on him?"

Ophelia was grateful that the dim light would mask her expression.

"We did find one blue thread," she admitted. "It should still be there near his right shoulder."

"Uh-huh." He shone the light over Septimus's clothes. Removing a pair of tweezers from his jacket he lifted the thread, placed it in a brown bag and put it in the pocket of his Mackintosh.

"Oh, and there is a tiny, amber jewel on the floor," she added. "It might possibly have dislodged from the jeweled dagger." She pointed and Southam flashed the torch causing the stone to glint. Pinching the stone with the tweezers, he held it up then pulled another small brown envelope from his pocket and slipped it inside.

"I won't be able to compare it with the jewels in the dagger until the doctor has examined the body. I assume he's on his way?"

"Should be here any minute, Inspector."

The inspector continued a thorough search.

"I wonder…?" Ophelia began.

He cocked a brow. "Yes?"

"We smelt the hint of vinegar on his sleeve."

The inspector leaned in to sniff the dead man's sleeves. "Yes, I can smell it too. Could mean he had fish and chips for supper."

"It could, except we don't have a fish and chip shop in the village and I don't believe Septimus had a car."

The inspector got to his feet with no small amount of grunting. "Before I take a look in this vault, I want a quick word with Constable Hargrove. Can you stay with the body?" Grinning he said, "Unless you're squeamish?"

"Not at all, Inspector."

The inspector disappeared in a flash, taking his torch with him and sinking the crypt into dim light once again.

The dead did not make for good company.

Ophelia began to walk around to give her mind something to do. As she rounded one of the tombs with its sculpted effigy, her shoe caught on something and she grabbed hold of the head of the supine statue. Looking down, she saw a discarded votive candle. Taking a handkerchief from her sleeve, she picked up the candle. It was worn half-way down, the sides bulging with solidified drips of wax.

The sudden sound of footsteps on the stairs shocked her and she almost dropped it.

"Ophelia!"

She let out a toxic sigh. "Over here, Imogen!"

"Tiger was fine and—oh! What do you have there?"

Ophelia presented the candle laying in the bed of handkerchief for her sister's perusal.

Imogen found her gaze. "Do you think it could be the candle used in the vault?"

"Hard to say. We are in a church, after all." She peered at it. "It does not look particularly old and there is no dust."

"Where's the inspector?" asked Imogen.

"He went to talk to Hargrove."

"Most of the choir has left now. The doctor is with Agatha."

The heavy crunch of shoes on the steps indicated the return of Inspector Southam.

"Alright, I'm ready to look in the vault now." The inspector stepped down into the treasury and swung the beam of his torch around the shadows. "Woah, it's like I'm in the ruddy British Museum!"

"It's mostly from the time of the Dissolution of the Monasteries by Henry VIII," explained Imogen. "It has been gathering dust for centuries."

The inspector pushed his hat back in wonder.

He ran back up the steps to take a look at the door. "They really should have a better lock on this place than that old flimsy thing. Anyone could pick it."

Ophelia glanced at her sister and put a finger to her lips.

"Where is the area the stuff was stolen from?" he asked.

The sisters moved ahead leading him to the very back of the vault.

"There," said Imogen, pointing.

The inspector whistled. "Frankly, I'm amazed he could tell."

"Like I said, he was a meticulous archivist," said Ophelia.

He scrunched his lips. "So, where's his record book?"

"Where indeed?" agreed Ophelia.

He tapped his notebook with a pencil. "Does Mr. Saville have an office?"

"I'm not sure. We'll need to ask the vicar," replied Ophelia.

The inspector flashed the beam over the pile of artifacts, down the side of the shelf and around the floor. "Is there anything else of interest down here?" He narrowed his eyes.

"Oh, yes! When Septimus brought us down here, we found a cassock stuffed over on that shelf," explained Imogen.

They both followed her and she reached for the garment that had been stashed.

"It's gone!" she gasped.

"Well, that's interesting," said Ophelia slowly.

"You're sure it was here?" Southam asked.

"Absolutely!" declared Ophelia. "We showed it to Septimus who said it wasn't his. He pointed out the difference between those he wears and the one we found. It was the kind monks wear."

"Our working theory is that whoever was stealing the items was disguising themselves in the cassock," explained Imogen. "Such an outfit would hide the person well and be unlikely to raise eyes around the church at odd hours."

The inspector scratched his head with the pencil. "Hmmm. Not a bad theory. So, whoever is stealing has now removed the cloak." He stood thinking, rubbing his chin. "I think it's time to look at the constable's notes."

"Uh—" said Imogen.

"Yes?"

"There is one more thing. We found a blob of wax on the floor near the shelf where the items were stolen."

The inspector scratched his cheek. "That could have been here for centuries before electricity was put in the place."

"It was recent. There was no dust or dirt on it," she responded.

"Let's have a look then."

Imogen reached into her handbag and handed the wax to the inspector who turned it over in his fingers.

"Perhaps Septimus used candles down here."

"No," contradicted Ophelia. "He had a splendid torch, better than yours, actually."

Inspector Southam took out a third brown bag. "But you have to admit that churches and candles kind of go together."

They all traipsed back up the stairs after securing the vault door.

Dr. Pemberton from Parkford was holding a drooping Agatha by the arm.

"Hello, Southam. I'm ready to examine the body but I've given this young lady here a sedative. She'll need someone to take her home."

"I can do that," said the vicar who had just entered the sanctuary.

"You'll have to talk to her some other time, Inspector," added the doctor. "She'll be out for the count in no time."

Chapter 12

Opening one weary eye, Imogen peeked at the clock, a gift from her children, that stood on the little table by her bed.

Nine o'clock!

She flung back the covers feeling slightly guilty.

Her mother's slipper chair sat snug against the window. Leaning over it, she opened the window wide and drank in the sweet, fresh air, letting the burble of the creek cover her with a blanket of security.

"Are you up, ducky?" called Ophelia.

The previous evening had been long and emotionally exhausting. They had both given statements to the constable, then sat up even later in their own kitchen discussing all the things they already knew about the awful crime and recording them in their special notebook. Cinderella would have been in trouble by the time they mounted the stairs.

Imogen let her head drop back. "Yes!"

"I've made you some eggs."

Imogen's stomach grumbled in response. "Coming!"

Slipping her narrow feet into worn slippers, she glanced at the treasures she had brought to Badger's Hollow. Two framed, juvenile drawings of the cottage from her grandchildren, a wedding picture on the chest of drawers, and a vial of sand from her honeymoon to Cornwall.

Winding down the stairs, she touched the little acorn doll from her youth.

Tiger leapt from his bed and nudged her legs.

"Good boy." She slid onto the chair as her sister placed a plate of sunny, yellow eggs and thick toast in front of her. "Thank you, lovey. Going to bed that late after all the excitement knocked me out."

"I'm wiped out too, but I couldn't sleep past seven," complained Ophelia. "Though I wanted to. I pottered around the kitchen garden and then got hungry."

Imogen took a bite of the eggs and closed her eyes with pleasure. "Ooh, thank you, lovey! It's so nice to have someone cook for me."

"And it's my pleasure to have someone to cook for," said Ophelia with a smile, bringing her cup of tea to the table.

"Mother was a great cook and took such delight in it. I never loved it but found myself cooking three square meals a day for forty odd years. That was one of the draws of going to live with Penny—I wouldn't have to cook anymore."

"You were a good cook, though," said Ophelia. "Even if you didn't like it."

"Well, that's as maybe but I'm glad to have retired from it and only cook the occasional tea cake when I choose to." She polished off the rest of the eggs. "Were you thinking about the murder when you couldn't sleep?"

"I suppose so." Ophelia withdrew the notebook she had used to organize their thoughts the night before. "I have been pondering the fact that we assumed the two types of theft are connected, but we actually have no evidence to support that. It could be two entirely different people. Then, working from assumption number one, we concluded that Septimus was killed because he interrupted the thief either going in or coming out of the vault. But to date, we only have circumstantial evidence that connects the thefts to the murder."

Imogen pushed her plate away. "I can't help feeling that if Septimus had gone to the police instead of us, he might still be alive."

"Uh-uh," replied Ophelia, shaking her head. "You can't play the 'what-if' game. There is only dissatisfaction at the end of that street." She went back to the notepad. "We also know that rigor had not set in and the blood was still flowing when Douglas found him, so the murder could not have happened that long before the choir practice was to begin."

"We watched everyone enter, since we were the first arrivals," said Imogen.

"Careful! That's another assumption. Other members of the choir could have been in the basement, slipped around the back and come in the door as if they had just arrived. Remember that the thief appears to be in the habit of stashing the cassock."

"You have a rather devious mind," Imogen grinned.

"I do, don't I?" Ophelia checked her notes again. "I'm taking Algernon off. He's far too feeble to attack someone and beat a hasty retreat up the stairs. If Septimus had been beaten with a cane, I might change my mind, but stabbing someone with a dagger seems too difficult for a man of his frailty."

"Agreed." Imogen poured herself another cup of tea. "Do you think that perhaps Agatha had a heart attack because she killed the man and it traumatized her?"

"If that were the case, I think her reaction would have occurred earlier. Remember, we began practice without Douglas. Agatha was fine as ninepence while we sang. It was only when she saw Douglas with bloodied hands that she took a turn."

"I wonder if she's alright this morning. I think the doctor gave her some kind of sedative and Harriet took her home."

"How about we go and visit the invalid in the spirit of compassion," suggested Ophelia with a twinkle in her eye.

Clutching a hastily cut bouquet of wildflowers, and Tiger's lead, the sisters knocked on Agatha Trumble's mean little cottage. The thatch was balding like a middle-aged man and the windows sagged like a drunk the morning after a binge.

"Oh!" Agatha's silver-streaked hair was sticking out at unnatural angles and she was still wearing a rather threadbare nightie. She stared down at Tiger with distaste. "Hello."

"May we come in, ducky? We've been so worried about you." Ophelia shouldered her way in as Agatha stepped back against a coat stand in bewilderment. Imogen and Tiger brought up the rear. The ingrained smell of mold tickled Imogen's nose and she quickly withdrew a scented handkerchief from her handbag.

Ophelia marched on, leading them into a cramped kitchen with peeling walls and rickety chairs.

"Shall I make us some tea?" asked Ophelia.

Poor Agatha was still in a daze.

Imogen closed the door to the kitchen and let Tiger off his lead. Tempted by the smorgasbord of unique scents he began a detailed inventory of the room.

"Uh, alright." Agatha ran a self-conscious hand over her wild hair.

While Ophelia bonged and banged the kettle and water, Imogen directed a sympathetic look at Agatha whose wrinkles began to dance as she struggled to hold back tears.

Touching her hand, Imogen began, "You seem deeply affected. Were you close to Septimus?"

Through misty eyes, Agatha shook her head. "I have an aversion to blood. Always have. You can imagine how that works in a school setting. Bloody noses, scraped knees to name just a few. It's awful. My emotions crescendo into a full-blown panic attack which manifests like a heart attack."

"I see. So, all that blood on Douglas set you off." This confirmed what they had already been told.

Agatha shuddered so hard the uneven chair rocked. "Uggh! It was horrible. Like a wretched nightmare. My brain descended into a chaos of fears and the attack took over."

The kettle was heating on the ancient stove top and Ophelia came to sit at the table. "What a dreadful curse." She patted the headmistress's hand. "How well *did* you know Septimus?"

Agatha's shoulders rose fractionally as her lips turned down. "I knew him in passing. He didn't sing in the choir and he wasn't married so he didn't have children at the school." She wiped her nose with a used, lacy handkerchief she pulled out of the sleeve of her billowing nightie.

"You really knew nothing else about him?" asked Imogen.

Agatha looked embarrassed. "Not really. I think he was good at his job as verger and I believe he lived in a cottage tied to the church." She waved the hankie. "I did hear a rumor he had a lady friend but I don't know who it was or if that was even true."

Imogen recognized the shift in her sister's eyes at this startling new revelation.

"If it is true, that person would be infinitely more affected by his passing than the rest of us," Ophelia mused. "And how long have you sung with the choir?"

Agatha shrugged again. "A long time. I don't really remember."

"More than five years? More than ten?" pushed Ophelia.

"Oh, more than ten."

"And when did your cousin join?"

A door slammed shut within Agatha. "Cousin?"

Imogen flapped her arms. "Oh, don't mind us. We're just playing catch-up on the village hierarchy. Perhaps we got the wrong end of the stick."

Agatha relaxed fractionally. "I forget that you grew up here." She crossed her arms. "If you are referring to Patricia Snodgrass, we do share a great-great-grandfather, but we don't really acknowledge the association."

"Families" began Ophelia. "They can be so complicated, can't they?"

Agatha bristled. "I wouldn't know."

"How long have *you* lived in this cottage?" asked Imogen. "It's very convenient for the school." She could see the edge of the little school building out of the back window of the kitchen.

"This tiny place actually belonged to my grandfather. He left it to my mother who already had a comfortable house, so it was rented out for many years." She tutted. "Renters! They just don't take care of a place like the owner does." Sniffing, she wiped her large nose. "When I first got the job as a teacher at the school my mother said I could live here. I put a lot of blood, sweat and tears in back then to return it to livable condition."

Imogen returned her gaze to the window over the sink, noticing it was held open with a chunk of wood. Looking around, she detected large damp stains on the ceiling and small patches of black mold.

"Of course, that was twenty years ago now and it could do with another facelift. The ravages of time and all that." Agatha blew her nose like a foghorn. "I don't have the energy I used to."

"I know just what you mean," agreed Ophelia. "We repainted Badger's Hollow from top to bottom. When I say 'we', I mean Harold's grandson. He was very professional and quick."

Slight pink blotches populated Agatha's cheeks. "On a teacher's salary I don't really have the means to pay a decorator."

"Perhaps we could organize the Women's Institute to help? Make it a work party?"

The pink deepened to fuchsia. "Oh, I couldn't take charity."

Imogen frowned. "It's not charity. Think of it as a group of your friends coming over to help with a project. They would do the same for anyone."

Agatha's thick lips twisted. "Maybe. I suppose I could buy the paint."

"I'll talk to Mildred, then." Mildred Chumbley was president of the Women's Institute.

"Alright. I still have a couple of weeks before school begins."

"I know from experience, thatched roofs are a beast to maintain. Mother said they needed to save for a long time when the thatch began to thin."

The kettle started to whistle and Ophelia stood to pour the boiling water into the tea pot. Tiger was still snuffling along the side of a chest.

"I can't even begin to *think* about fixing the roof. Instead, I've invested in a dozen pails to catch the leaks when it rains."

Ophelia brought the teapot, cups and saucers to the table on a tray with some milk. "Oh, how inconvenient! And it makes the place so damp. That would bother Imogen's arthritic shoulder terribly."

"It doesn't help me any, either. The humid air burrows into my joints and really slows me down," responded Agatha.

Ophelia poured the tea. "You might need to consider taking out a loan with the bank for something as costly as that."

Tiger must have found a mouse or something and was wiggling his posterior with vigor.

The crimson tint returned to Agatha's skin with a vengeance. "Oh, I don't know—"

Tiger reared back, clutching something between his giant jaws.

He laid it at Imogen's feet with an expression of utter adoration and satisfaction as Agatha leaned forward with an ear-splitting screech.

It was a receipt for £50.

Chapter 13

"I-I can explain," Agatha stuttered.

Tiger continued to look extremely pleased with himself as the twins merely stared at the receipt.

Agatha bowed her head and began to pulverize the hankie. "A friend introduced me to the horses at Epsom Downs a few years ago. I got caught up in the glamor, the atmosphere, the glitz. I even spotted the Prince of Wales." She wiped away a tear. "Anyway, I put a trifle on a horse. I had no idea what I was doing and I put it on a horse that had absolutely no chance of winning. Except it did. I can't adequately describe the thrill that powered through me like a bolt of lightning. I was hooked. I immediately put all the money I won onto other horses...and lost the lot. But all I could think of was experiencing that thrill again." She got up from the table and began to pace.

"My extended family doesn't know about my...problem. That's why I stash the evidence away. I'm rather ashamed really. That receipt is for some of my mother's jewelry. I pawned it in Parkford for a day at the races back in June. I just know if I could pick the right horse, my money woes would be over. Don't you see?" The look of giddy hope burning in her face was heart-breakingly pathetic.

"Agatha," began Imogen in a tone she had used many times with her children. "You are an intelligent woman. You *know* that gambling will not solve your problems. It rather sounds like you need help to overcome this addiction."

"Oh, it's not an addiction!" cried Agatha, grabbing the back of her chair so savagely her knuckles turned white.

"Then what would you call it?" asked Imogen, quietly.

One of Agatha's infant class pupils could not have looked more forlorn on the first day of school. "A guilty pleasure?"

"Is that not the real reason you have no funds to fix your house?" asked Ophelia.

"No! Yes." Agatha sank onto the chair, hands covering her face. She was a woman on the edge of an emotional cliff.

Imogen moved to sit beside the distraught headmistress and placed an arm around her shaking shoulders. "There, there. I imagine admitting you have a problem is the first step. I'd be happy to check on you from time to time to provide some accountability."

Like a lamb saved from the slaughter, Agatha asked, "Would you? I used to look down my nose at gamblers." She snapped up her large head, cheeks shining. "You won't tell anyone will you? I can't bear anyone else knowing I have this weakness. I would almost certainly lose my position as head of the school."

Ophelia tapped the side of her nose. "You can trust us."

Once outside the ramshackle dwelling, with a loping Tiger straining on the lead at their side, Ophelia said, "You know, we only have *her* word that she sold her mother's jewelry for that cash. It could very easily have been candlesticks from the church."

Imogen stopped and Tiger followed suit looking up at her with expectation.

"I hadn't thought of that." She fed Tiger a treat for stopping from her pocket.

"You're far too trusting, ducky."

Imogen chewed on the thought for a few minutes, then asked, "What next?"

"I want to see Douglas. He found the body. He might have noticed things he doesn't even realize. He should be less distraught today."

The door of the Horton-Black's cottage was opened by a dramatically diminished Gladys.

"How is Douglas?" began Imogen. "We wanted to check that he is recovering from his shock."

Gladys set her eyes on Tiger and pulled the door closed behind her as she leant on her cane.

"Oh, he's very bad," she moaned. "He hasn't been able to get out of bed. And the nightmares. It was awful."

"Perhaps you should call the doctor. He might be able to prescribe something for him," suggested Ophelia.

"I tried but he won't have it. Just says he needs time."

"What did he tell you?" pushed Ophelia.

"That he went to get some additional choir music from the cupboard in the crypt and tripped over something. Then to his horror, he saw Septimus laying lifeless in a pool of blood." Gladys put a hand to her mouth to stop a sob. "How does one recover from something like that?"

There was no good answer, so the twins remained silent.

"He tried to get the knife out. That's how he got blood all over himself," Gladys explained. "Seeing all that blood on his hands he passed out and cracked his head on the stone floor. Oh!" she wailed. "What is the world coming to?"

It was clear that the couple were too traumatized to make good witnesses today. Imogen squeezed Gladys's hand. "We'll stop by another day."

♪♪

"Poor thing. It's going to take them a while to shake this off," declared Imogen as they left.

"Yes," replied Ophelia, dragging out the vowel. "Let's take Tiger home. Remember how the inspector said he had not found Septimus's notebook? I want to go and poke around his cottage."

"Oh, no! Are we breaking in again? I don't think my nerves can take it," asked Imogen, recalling when they were caught red-handed trespassing in a victim's home.

"No! I'm going to ask the vicar for the key."

"Thank heavens!"

♪♪

The vicarage was bustling with activity. The vicar's daughter was dressed for tennis while her mother, Prudence called for their son to hurry.

"Is the vicar home?" Ophelia asked the girl.

"Daddy!" she shrieked as if she were a sailor in a storm on deck, pushing past them and out onto the gravel drive.

Imogen blinked hard.

"Oh, hello," said Prudence, pounding down the stairs to the entry. "I'm afraid I'm popping out with the kiddies."

"We're here to see your husband, actually," explained Ophelia.

"Here for me?" The vicar appeared, face strained with grief, his shirt sleeves rolled up. "Please excuse my relaxed appearance." His whole countenance was world-weary. "I'm planning the funeral for Septimus."

Prudence pursed her lips and stiffly kissed her husband's cheek. "Sorry to dash, darling," she said. "But we're running late." As she spoke, their boy, about nine, jumped down the last four stairs with a bump and ran outside without even acknowledging their presence.

The vicar's neck sank into his dog collar. "Sorry about that."

"Boys will be boys," said Imogen.

He rubbed his hands together. "What can I do for you?"

"We'd like to look around Septimus's cottage and were hoping you would give us the key."

His mournful face stiffened like a wooden mask. "Uh–if you don't mind me saying so, I'm not sure that would be quite appropriate. And besides, the police have already searched it."

Ophelia raised a hand in objection. "We didn't tell you this yesterday, Vicar, but Septimus had asked us to look into something and now he's dead. I believe that endows us with the authority you're looking for."

The mask fell, dissolved by shock. "What?"

"He approached us after our first choir practice."

"What was it about…if I may ask?"

Ophelia bit her lip. "It's…complicated. He wanted to keep it confidential until we had concluded our investigation."

"Investigation? But now he's dead, does it matter?"

"I rather think it does," she argued. "Until we can categorically say that his death is not linked to the other matter, I would rather keep it under my hat if you don't mind."

Reverend Cresswell's face clouded again. "But—"

"The matter would require you to make an official report to your superiors, if Septimus is proven correct."

Comprehension blossomed over the vicar's plain features. "Oh."

"As soon as we draw any conclusions, you will be the first to know—well, the second. We should probably inform the inspector first."

"Does the inspector know what the matter is about?"

"Yes," replied Imogen. "We told him all about it. He doesn't have to report it in the same way you would."

The stress betrayed by the lines on the vicar's face, kicked up a notch. "Should I worry? Will I get into trouble?"

The twins glanced at each other. "I don't honestly know," said Ophelia. "But we cannot tip the perpetrator off at this point, in case it is the reason Septimus was murdered."

"I see." Reverend Cresswell dropped his glance to the floor then looked up with decision. "Just a moment."

Still standing on the doorstep, the sisters looked around the wide entrance hall of the parsonage. A beautiful, ornamental cross stood on an occasional table next to a vase of dried flowers. Several pairs of shoes were scattered underneath the table and a ball trapped between its legs. A gilded mirror hung where the stairs began, several landscape paintings running up the wall.

Upon his return, the vicar's hair was mussed, and a deep wrinkle of tension stretched between his eyes.

"I wish Septimus had come straight to me. I thought we were good friends. I might have been able to prevent his death."

"Don't waste any concern on that front," assured Imogen. "He came to us to *save* you from worry *because* you were his friend. His hope was that we could clean up the problem with you none the wiser."

The vicar nodded and handed over the key.

"Do you know if he was seeing anyone?" asked Ophelia, remembering Agatha's comment.

The vicar's green eyes flashed with a hint of humor. "I did get that impression, though he never told me in so many words."

They turned to leave but Ophelia spun back. "Do you happen to have his treasury record book?"

"No. The inspector asked me the same thing. I've seen it, of course, but no."

The verger's tiny cottage was built in the same style as the church, rather than the rest of the dwellings in the village. An austere stone box, it wore a slate tile roof. Two small windows sat either side of the front door. The only color was from the late summer flowers blooming in a neatly trimmed flower bed.

Imogen pushed the key into the shiny, black door and pushed. The mid-afternoon sun blasted through the back windows, smacking them in the face. Shielding their eyes, they blinked frantically as Imogen ran to pull the curtains.

Once they had recovered the power of sight, they saw that the front door opened straight into an immaculate, modest sitting room behind which was a scrupulously clean kitchen table, a tidy sink and a large fireplace for cooking.

Not a speck of dust resided anywhere.

The faint smell of disinfectant mingled with tobacco, still lingered.

The furnishings were spartan and dated but clean as a whistle. Pushing through into the kitchen area, a small opening in the wall revealed a tiny bedroom housing a simple, narrow bed, high window, and a pitcher and bowl. No bathroom.

Imogen moved back into the kitchen area and pulling back the curtain saw the sharp edges of an outhouse at the bottom of an immaculate garden.

"I'll start in here," said Ophelia walking into the bedroom. "You look in the kitchen."

Nothing was out of place. Even the wooden cutting board had been rigorously cleaned and stored. A cast iron pot hung from the hook over the fire but it was as clean as the day the smithy had forged it. A small cabinet sat in the corner of the kitchen with a stack of bowls and some metal cutlery, and on top rested a pristine pipe in a glistening ashtray.

She moved to the sitting room. Two old-fashioned armchairs sat either side of a smaller fireplace. Their cherry wood arms gleamed in the sunlight. An oak occasional table beside one of the chairs was bare; no photographs or knick-knacks.

"I found something," called Ophelia from the bedroom.

In five steps, Imogen was there.

"Love letters!" declared Ophelia.

Chapter 14

"Love letters?" Imogen thought of the non-descript, middle-aged man with a fetish for order. "Who are they from?"

"They aren't signed," explained Ophelia, lifting a stack of letters bound by a loose red ribbon. She flourished one. "I can tell the police have already been through them because the pile is messy. But they are written in the tidiest handwriting I have ever seen. It almost looks like they were printed. It's obviously someone with a penchant for orderliness as acute as his."

Imogen took the anonymous letter from her sister. The penmanship was of the highest quality. A Franciscan monk would have been proud of the work.

July 20, 1928

The letter was quite recent. She began to read it aloud.

Lambkin,
I do love nothing in the world so well as you.

"That's Shakespeare," declared Ophelia with authority.

Imogen continued to read.

I do love you more than words can wield the matter. You will never age for me, nor fade, nor die.

"That too," added Ophelia.

Love is not love when it alteration finds, and mine for you alters not.
Doubt that the sun doth move
Doubt truth to be a liar
But never doubt I love.
Ladybird.

"It's a mishmash. Terms of endearment pulled from various Shakespearean works." Ophelia pulled her mouth down. "Sweet, but not original."

Imogen lifted her face, emblazoned with a blissful smile as though she were sixteen again and had just experienced her first kiss. "*I* think it's terribly romantic." She hugged the letter to her chest.

"If you say so." Ophelia flicked through the other letters. "No proper signature on any of them. Just 'Ladybird'."

"What was the first one like?"

Ophelia handed it to Imogen.

Angel,

You cannot know how thy words have delighted and stirred my soul.

Never has man compared me to a summer's day as thou hast.

With your words you own me. One half of me is yours, the other half yours

Come, woo me, woo me.

I would not wish

Any companion in the world but you

Ladybird

Imogen sighed.

"Sounds as though Septimus made the first move," said Ophelia. "Though it's hard to imagine him as a Romeo."

"Since the letters are anonymous, it is possible that they remained secret admirers," posited Imogen.

Ophelia clapped. "You mean, they were each unaware of who their secret love was?"

"Obviously, Septimus knew, if we are correct in deducing that he started this romance. But if he did not reveal his identity before his untimely death, the woman may still not know who it was." She grabbed her gold locket. "Which is truly sad as the letters will just stop."

"I wonder how they exchanged the letters?"

"That would be interesting to know," mused Imogen. "I'm guessing you didn't find any kind of diary in his bedroom."

"No. Scrupulous as Septimus was, he did not record his daily life."

"And no ledger of the church artifacts?"

"No," replied Ophelia. "I assume the murderer stole it."

"Drat! But that does make sense." Imogen handed the letter back. "Nonetheless, finding these letters may be helpful. We can ask Celina if anyone has checked out any Shakespeare from the library recently."

"And snagging samples of various women's handwriting might be useful, too."

♪

The tiny library was a village hub. When the twins arrived, it was crowded with mothers and children finding books to fill the remaining days of the summer holidays.

A small line of people waited to check out their finds, and the sisters joined the back of the queue.

Celina was quite clearly in her element. She had been the assistant librarian until her boss had been arrested for murder. Though quite young, she was obviously well equipped to take on running the place.

When they reached her desk, she looked at their empty hands with confusion.

"We need some information," Imogen explained.

Celina raised both brows.

"Has anyone been checking out Shakespearean works this year?"

Celina smiled, sadly. "Don't you know that already? It was Septimus."

Ophelia's heart rate shot up. "Did he mention why?"

"Not really. Just said he had developed an interest." She leaned forward. "Why? Do you know something?"

"It's a line of investigation. We don't have enough of the dots connected to share our theory just yet," said Ophelia.

Celina's face fell.

"No one else has taken a recent interest in Shakespeare?" pushed Imogen.

Celina shook her head. "No. In these modern times there's not really a call for the Bard."

"How are you settling into your new job?" asked Imogen.

"Between you and me, Connie was a bit behind the times in the world of library science. It has been quite liberating to be in charge."

"And the increase in salary must be a nice bonus," added Ophelia, since Celina was on their list of suspects.

It was not very British to speak of such private things as salaries and Celina's face clouded. "Indeed."

"I didn't mean to pry. Just put it down to me being a nosy old lady," blustered Ophelia in an effort to diffuse the awkward situation.

The people behind them were getting restless.

"Anyway, thanks for the info. We'll be seeing you," said Imogen.

A puffy cloud blotted the sun as they stepped out of the library.

"What were you thinking?" asked Imogen.

"The opportunity presented itself and I took it." Ophelia's tone was defensive.

"Well, at least it confirms that Septimus was using Shakespeare's texts as the basis for his own letters," said Imogen.

"What I'd really love to know is, *who* was the object of his passion and *how* it all started," said Ophelia, adjusting her hat.

"That is something we may never know," sighed Imogen. "But did you see the handwritten note on Celina's desk? It was neat handwriting but nothing like the quality of that in the letters."

♫

They had been away from home for quite some time and were eager to get back to Tiger before he tore the place apart. Arriving at the village green, they began to cross it as a shortcut to Badger's Hollow. Deep in conversation about daggers, missing ledgers, and love letters they did not notice someone approaching from the opposite direction.

"Miss Harrington."

Ophelia stopped abruptly.

Standing before them was a bald, husky man in his mid-sixties who bore more than a passing resemblance to their butcher.

Imogen let slip a gasp.

"Mrs. Pettigrew."

"Jeffrey," replied Imogen.

"I was hoping I might bump into you. How have you been, Ophelia?"

Imogen could feel the distress rippling off her sister in tidal waves.

"Quite well," she replied stiffly, looking everywhere but at him. "And you? I heard your wife died. I'm sorry."

"Thank you," he replied. "Her illness was thankfully of short duration and we had a simple but happy life." He clasped his hands together. "She taught me the breadth of a woman's abilities, Ophelia."

Ophelia's rigid shoulders dropped. "Really?"

"Yes. We attended several of your orchestral concerts in London. We followed your career. Martha was thrilled that women were being recognized as professional artists. She put our Lillian in violin lessons and Bobby played the piano. They were never as good as you, but they had some talent."

"Imogen, why don't you go and see to Tiger while I visit with Jeffrey?"

"Are you sure?" Imogen tried to read her sister's mind.

Ophelia reached out and grabbed Imogen's hand. "I'm sure."

"It was nice to see you, Jeffrey."

He tipped his hat as Imogen continued across the green.

"Shall we sit?" said Ophelia pointing to the bench her father had donated to the village, heart pounding in her chest.

"What brought you back to Saffron Weald?" he asked. She knew he must have been told the reasons by his brother but appreciated his effort to break the thick iceberg between them. She gave him an abridged version of events.

"Did you like Colchester?" she asked when she was done.

He gave her the side-eye. "Anything was better than Saffron Weald at the time."

She pursed her lips. "I'm sorry for the way I broke things off."

"I'm sorry I was so pig-headed. I couldn't see the world was changing and that my ideas on a woman's place were becoming old-fashioned." He placed his arm along the back of the bench, bridging the gap between them. "The irony is that Martha liked the opera. She dragged me along saying it would be good for me."

Ophelia shifted in her seat. "Did you begin to appreciate it?"

"I could lie and say yes. But the truth was, I did it to please her. I got to where I didn't hate it anymore."

Ophelia blew air through her nose. "That's progress, from what I remember."

He chuckled. "I was an unsophisticated bull in my youth. I let pride blind me. But I do believe I'm a better man today." He smiled. "Tell me about your life. I want to hear it all."

She told him of her move to London, her life there, living alone on a small allowance from her parents. She described teaching violin lessons to make ends meet, of the creation of the women's orchestra and securing a place in it. Of her travels to the far corners of the earth.

"I would have held you back," he admitted. "As progressive as I am now in comparison, you wouldn't have experienced all that if you'd married me."

A blanket of peace enveloped her.

"How did you meet Martha?" she asked.

He filled her in on his own life. How he had met his wife at a local dance about six months after fleeing to Colchester. He explained that she was born and bred in the area and upon learning he was new, promised to show him all the delights of that part of the county.

"She was a traditional girl. All she wanted was to be a wife and mother, scattered with the odd cultural event. That suited me down to the ground. But she was refined in some ways—like her interest in the opera. Martha felt that people should try to improve themselves." He wiped his eye.

"After we'd been married a couple of years, she asked why I'd left Meadowshire. I told her everything. Years later, we saw your name in the paper as a member of that orchestra and she said we had to go."

"I'm honored," she replied, truthfully. "You should have waited for me after the performance. I'd have liked to meet her."

He shook his head. "My heart was settled. I didn't want to stir things up."

She let the comment sink in for a minute.

"And what profession did you take up?" she finally asked.

He chuckled. "You're not going to believe this after my storming out of here in a huff, but I became a butcher. It was all I knew and an elderly butcher in Colchester needed a young assistant. I eventually took over from him. My son runs the place with me now."

He looked up, stricken with anxiety.

"I've always felt bad about the way things ended. I came to Saffron Weald with the intention of making amends."

She touched his hand with a finger. "I'd say you accomplished that very nicely."

Chapter 15

On Thursday morning they received two messages. Douglas sent a note that choir practice was canceled as he was still feeling wobbly and the inspector called to let them know that Reginald Tumblethorn, Archie Puddingfield, Arabella Fudgeford, Harriet Cleaver, the colonel and the vicar's wife, all had solid alibis. After making a note of this new information, the postman arrived with some music Ophelia had ordered and since it would keep her busy for the next couple of hours, Imogen thought it a good time to make a cake for their choir master who had been so unhinged by his grisly experience.

Holding the freshly baked coffee cake, Imogen knocked on the door of the Horton-Black's cottage. A heavy plodding noise preceded the opening of the door, to reveal Douglas's wife, Gladys, with her cane.

"Oh, you shouldn't have!" she declared in her delightful northern accent, focusing on the cake with a greedy eye. "Come in, come in. Your sister not with you?"

"She got some new music and wanted to tackle it."

"Oh, so *you* are Mrs. Pettigrew." Gladys dipped her chin. "I feel embarrassed to admit it but I can't tell the two of you apart." Mrs. Horton-Black had not grown up in the village and was several years younger than the twins.

"Don't be embarrassed. It happens all the time," Imogen assured her.

She followed Gladys down the neat hallway littered with pictures of cats and pastoral scenes and into the spacious drawing room where the audition had taken place.

"I'll just go and put the kettle on. Be back in a jiffy."

Imogen settled herself into a chair and put the cake on the coffee table. Left alone, she noticed things she hadn't the first time. Certificates of achievement in music hung proudly on one wall, a set of first editions took up two rows of an oak bookcase, an old, hand drawn map graced another wall, flanked by the framed teaching diplomas of both Douglas and his wife. There was even a commendation for bravery in WWI on the fireplace.

"The kettle's on," said Gladys coming back into the room with a bright smile. "Douglas should be back any minute. He popped out to get some bread."

A cat appeared from under the chair and jumped onto Gladys's knee. "Did you meet Spartacus last time? He doesn't like the loud music, so he hides in the bedroom. But he's a darling."

The cat turned suspicious eyes on Imogen and she felt a quiver of apprehension.

"I can't believe all that's happened since you were here last," said Gladys. "That poor Mr. Saville, who never hurt anyone. What *is* the world coming to? Douglas has hardly slept a wink since finding him. He thinks I don't know, but I hear him pacing the floor at two in the morning. When he does finally fall asleep, he has nightmares. Just like after the war."

"I shouldn't wonder," said Imogen. "We're all very shaken by the tragedy, but Douglas was the unfortunate one who found the body."

The kettle began to sing. "Be back in a jiffy!"

The cat eyed Imogen, sniffing the air. Picking up Tiger's scent he stalked away, tail high. Imogen's gaze fell on the old map. She rose to examine it and for the first time realized that it was a map of Saffron Weald.

A bump against the door indicated that Gladys was back with the tea and Imogen rushed to her aid, taking the tea tray and setting it next to the cake.

Once they were both seated again, Gladys reached for the teapot and winced with pain.

"Here, let me do that," said Imogen.

"How kind. My back is really acting up at the moment."

"Is there anything that can be done?"

"I'm seeing a specialist. There's an experimental surgery that might help but I'm nervous about doing it."

"That's understandable." Imogen knocked on the wooden table. "I've been really fortunate. I've never had to go to the hospital."

Gladys suddenly looked wrung out like an old rag. "That is extremely lucky. I feel like I've been in and out since I contracted polio."

The front door blew open. "Gladys!"

"In here, Doug."

Not expecting a visitor, he jumped a little upon seeing Imogen. "Good afternoon, Mrs. Pettigrew." He spotted the cake. "Is that by any chance your mother's famous coffee cake?" Imogen noted that his color was better and that he seemed almost back to his old self.

"It certainly is, though I can't claim it will be as good as hers."

Douglas clapped his hands. "Let me put this stuff away and I'll join both of you."

What with one thing and another, the next time the twins made it to the church was for their inaugural Sunday School class. They entered the classroom containing four pint-sized chairs with some trepidation.

One little girl wriggled in her seat then pulled her dress right over her head revealing much more of next week's washing than was decent. The boy next to her picked his nose, his clear hazel eyes not leaving Ophelia's. Another girl with red pigtails smiled sweetly, revealing a gap in her front teeth, and a boy with dark curls and piercing blue eyes offset by a brush of freckles, swung his legs. Prudence Cresswell had assured them they had been given the best-behaved class, but Ophelia was beginning to wonder.

Of the opinion that Imogen had prepared far too many activities, Ophelia was more than grateful they had enough to keep the young children's attention after a rather rocky start.

Exhausted and feeling in dire need of immediate refreshment after class ended, they hobbled over to the church for the worship service. The vicar still looked peaky, and his sermon lacked its usual vigor. More than once Imogen felt herself nod off and Ophelia's dry mouth and scratchy throat made it difficult for her to sing. She was thankful the choir was not performing as part of the service today.

By their second cup of tea in fellowship hall, they were feeling restored when the vicar came over to sit by them.

"I have to tell you, I've been up at night wondering what Septimus came to you about," he began, his pointed nose quivering with inquisitiveness. "Is it something that places my congregation in danger?" He made a bridge with his long fingers. "I feel a keen responsibility for the welfare of my flock, you know." None of the vicar's features offered a sense of completion and as such were unable to conjure up any sort of determined expression.

A slight tip of the head from Imogen signaled Ophelia to take over the conversation.

"Obviously, there has been a murder," she began. "A violent act of aggression. However, we are of the opinion that Septimus may just have been in the wrong place at the wrong time. A deadly coincidence, if you will. We don't believe the murderer was loitering with the intent to commit the deed against Septimus. Does that ease your concerns, Reverend Cresswell?"

He ran a hand down his homely face. "A little, I suppose. Did you find anything useful at his cottage?"

They had decided to keep the information about the love letters to themselves for the time being. "Septimus was an immaculate housekeeper with very few personal items," responded Ophelia. "Do you know anything of his background?"

"He grew up in an orphanage in Sussex. He was given the name Septimus because he was the seventh baby boy to be left there that year. A man without roots." He pressed his fingers together. "You may be interested to know that he was an amateur philosopher. We spent many an evening talking in intellectual circles. I enjoyed his company and he was excellent at his job. I never had to worry about the regalia or artifacts for the worship service. He took care of everything." The crack in the vicar's voice betrayed how deeply he felt the loss of his friend. "The cottage, a home of his own, meant everything to the boy who grew up without one."

Given the vicar's affection for the victim, Ophelia had a change of heart and resolved to take the vicar into their confidence. "Do you remember us asking if there was a lady in his life?" asked Ophelia, quietly. "You thought perhaps he was gearing up to take the plunge. The truth was, he had already dived in headfirst."

The vicar's head dipped. "Really?"

"Yes! He was rather a dark horse, it seems," Imogen added. "We found a stack of love letters in the most incredible handwriting you ever saw, from his lady friend."

Bartholomew Cresswell leaned his tall body back in his chair. "You could blow me over with a feather. Who is it?"

Imogen folded her arms. "Unfortunately, they were anonymous. Dating back to early this summer."

The vicar closed his eyes then stabbed the air with a finger. "That's it!"

The twins shared a confused look.

"He would come over on Tuesday evenings to go over church business. After it was completed, we would sit in the easy chairs in my study and he would smoke his pipe. Over a glass of whiskey, we delved into philosophical discussions. He was a fairly serious fellow—probably the result of a difficult childhood—but in late May, I noticed a subtle difference. He was lighter, happier. I mentioned the change in his countenance but he blew it off, ascribing it to the coming of summer. Romance must have been the real reason." The vicar tapped his chin. "A lady friend. Imagine that."

Ophelia dunked a biscuit in her tea. "We all need our secrets and a little excitement in our lives, Vicar. And now that we know more about Septimus, romance was probably a brand new world. A completely new sensation. And, we're not sure the lady in question even knew it was him at the time of his death."

"Really?"

"The letters he received were unsigned which leads us to suppose that *his* letters to her were also anonymous," said

Ophelia. "Can you imagine leading an incredibly small life, then experiencing the explosion of a secret relationship?"

Rubbing his ear, the vicar remarked, "I remember when I met Pru. She was a vision and I was sure I didn't stand a chance. I mean, look at me. But I could barely conceal all the emotions igniting inside my heart."

"The letters to Septimus were not traditional love letters," explained Imogen. "They were constructed purely of quotes from Shakespeare. We checked with the librarian; Septimus had been checking out such books himself."

"What a love story," the vicar sighed.

"One that came to a screeching and untimely end," pointed out Imogen. "I don't suppose you know of any ladies in your flock who are partial to the Bard?"

Dull eyes rolled up to the right as he considered. "I don't. Even our amateur dramatics society doesn't wade into Shakespeare."

"Morning!" bellowed Mildred as she sat down at their table uninvited, sloshing her tea on to the saucer, bringing their confidential conversation to a grinding halt. "You all looked like you were having a lively discussion and I thought, Mildred! You *must* know what they are talking about." As the village gossip, Mildred inserted herself into many exchanges that were rolling along happily without her.

"Well, I should spread myself out," said the vicar, hastily rising to his large feet. He bowed. "Ladies."

"What do you think of Shakespeare?" asked Imogen with a pointed glance at her sister. "That's what we were talking about."

Mildred's uncomely nose wrinkled. "I'm not a fan myself. I've seen the odd production in town, but I find the language a bit tricky."

"Do all your friends feel the same way?" *Friends* was pushing it. Most people spent their time trying to avoid Mildred.

She flapped her hand. "I would say so. It's the kind of thing they force on you at school that no one really likes, isn't it?"

Though Ophelia had resolute opinions on the topic, she did not want to waste them on Mildred.

"Do you know anything more about the murder?" Mildred asked, her back hunched as if to provide a wall of secrecy between them and the rest of the crowd in the hall. "Are you involved again?"

"We were at the choir practice when the body was discovered," said Imogen.

"Yes, I heard you'd joined the choir," Mildred sniffed. "Although I was hoping one of you would join the bell ringers, I suppose it's a good fit with your background." She took a sip. "I heard Septimus was stabbed by a vagrant living in the crypt, with a religious dagger."

"I don't know where you heard that," responded Ophelia sharply. "But that is total fiction."

"Even the part about the dagger?"

"No, the bit about the vagrant."

"So, he *was* stabbed with a dagger belonging to the church," she cried triumphantly. "What was the motive, do you think?"

Hot crumpets! Mildred had played them.

"The police have not released a motive," responded Ophelia.

"The police, the police. What good are they? You were the ones who brought Connie to justice. You must have *some* theories about this."

"Sadly, we know very little." Ophelia was prevaricating and judging by the twist of Mildred's mouth, it was obvious.

"But you *are* investigating?" Desperation was getting the better of Mildred, beads of sweat popping out of every pore on the tip of her nose.

"Well, we *were* there. And we were acquainted with the victim, but it's all unofficial." Ophelia was beginning to enjoy the feeling of one-upmanship over Mildred. It was like a shot of pure glee.

With a great deal of effort, Mildred swallowed and rearranged her cup, bringing her fervor for gossip down to measurable levels. "I heard Douglas staggered in dripping with blood."

"Is that really the tone of conversation suited to a village hall after church?" asked Imogen with no small dose of revulsion.

Shoulders waggling with indignation like a hen whose chicks are threatened, Mildred blurted out, "Well, the murder happened right here in the church, didn't it?"

She had a point.

"Correct but is it appropriate to bring it up?" asked Ophelia.

Crossing her arms, Mildred glared. "Did it happen or not? I think I have a right to know what happens in my own church."

"Douglas tried to help Septimus…" Ophelia stopped. Douglas had no corroborating witness to confirm his story. She tried to imagine him taking the dagger and plunging it into Septimus's back. Just as quickly, she remembered that he passed out, smacking his head on the hard crypt floor. "… and got blood on his hands in the effort. Poor thing. It turned his stomach so badly he blacked out and bashed his head. He's still not well."

"I shouldn't wonder," cried Mildred. "It would have sent me to the asylum."

Her undisguised, breathless excitement was disgusting.

"Was it really a dagger from the church's own collection?" she continued.

"The police have not confirmed the fact, but it does seem to be the case." This reminded Ophelia that they really needed that inventory ledger to check if there was a jeweled dagger among its pages. And what about that loose precious stone? Was it from the dagger? They needed to talk to the inspector.

Mildred continued, like a broken sewer. "I heard Agatha had one of her turns. I think they're getting worse. She'll lose her job if she's not careful and we *all* know she needs it."

Imogen's biscuits sat heavy in her stomach.

"Do you have any suspects?" Mildred's eyes darted between them.

It was time to go.

"We're not really comfortable with saying anything at this point," said Imogen, pushing the rest of her biscuits away.

"You don't really know anything, do you?" Mildred accused. "I knew last time was a fluke. Lucky guess. Now everyone thinks you're the bee's knees."

Ophelia was feeling claustrophobic.

"And a little bird told me *you* had a tête à tête with Jeffrey Cleaver. I'm surprised given that he cast you off as a girl—"

This was the last straw. "Mildred!" roared Imogen, standing over her. "That is enough! Come, Ophelia. We must see to Tiger."

Struck into stunned silence as though Mildred had physically slapped her across the face, Ophelia allowed herself to be led away. *Was nothing sacred?*

They left without saying goodbye and Ophelia whispering, "I take no leave of your mother…"

Chapter 16

Distressed by the stormy confrontation with Mildred, they hurried home. Ophelia immediately whipped out her violin. Imogen sat in a chair by the empty fire waiting for the storm inside to subside, while Tiger laid his head peacefully on her lap.

Though Mildred possessed the tact of a gnat, some of her points could not be easily dismissed and had stirred up some valid questions in Imogen's mind. How would the inspector feel about sharing information with them? He might be more willing if they offered a quid pro quo. Perhaps a conversation about the love letters might be enough.

Imogen hesitated. It was Sunday. Did inspectors keep office hours or was it an all-hands-on-deck situation with murder? As she sat pondering, Tiger jerked his head, a low growl sounding in the back of his throat. A second later, a knock on the door sent Tiger into full throttle. Ophelia, ignoring the bedlam, continued to play.

"Inspector Southam! I was just thinking of you!" Imogen pulled Tiger back by his collar.

The inspector's lips curled into a smile. "I don't know whether to be flattered or worried. May I come in?"

Tiger stopped his barking but did not take his active eyes off the policeman.

"Where are my manners? Of course!" replied Imogen.

Upon seeing the inspector, Ophelia dropped the violin from her neck, holding the bow up like a weapon.

"Good afternoon, Miss Harrington. I hope I'm not disturbing you?"

She laid the instrument and bow on top of the piano. "Not at all, Inspector. How can we help you?" She took the chair across from her sister and gestured to the sofa.

"I was in the village on police business and thought I'd check in since you are 'in situ'." He raised his brows. "I wondered if you might have anything to share."

As Imogen watched the inspector and her sister, she had the sudden impression of fighters sparring, each waiting for the opponent to make the first move.

"In consideration of the fact that Septimus had approached us about the thefts, the vicar allowed us access to his cottage," offered Ophelia. "After your men had been through it, of course."

A flicker of an eyebrow indicated irritation. "Precious lot of evidence we found there. The man lived like a monk and was more house proud than my mother." He tipped his head. "Unless you found something we missed?"

"You did not find the love letters in the least interesting?" Ophelia asked him.

The inspector huffed. "It was all gobbledygook to me. Couldn't make head nor tail of it. And they weren't signed. We took a couple for fingerprint testing, but the results were inconclusive."

Ophelia clasped her hands together and placed them on her knee. "But they do indicate the existence of a sweetheart. Another person to add to the pool of suspects."

Tiger wandered over to the inspector who raised a hand to pat his head. "Well," he blustered. "That much is true. But I've asked around, and no one seems to know anything about it. Certainly, no one is admitting to being the lady in question."

Rather than criticize his bull in a china shop tactics, Imogen said, "The relationship was obviously secret. I daresay it added to the thrill. However, only a fool would not realize they'd be considered a suspect in his death."

"Have you conducted a handwriting comparison?" asked Ophelia.

He shifted in his seat. "Not at this point. I'm concentrating my inquiries around those who sing in the choir." He looked up sharply. "Do *you* know who the mystery woman is?"

"Alas, not yet. But we're making some progress. The gobbledygook, as you call it, is Shakespeare. We checked with Celina at the library and she confirmed that Septimus had been checking out his plays and poetry. We hope it's only a matter of time until we find a lady who is an equal enthusiast."

"Time is a luxury I have little of," he said with a frown. "Will you let me know the minute you find something?"

"Of course," said Ophelia with the smile that Imogen recognized as her flytrap. "Might we ask *you* some questions?"

"As long as you understand there may be some I am not at liberty to answer."

"Naturally." She reclasped her hands. "Did you happen to find Septimus's ledger of the treasures in the crypt?"

"Blast it! No." Tiger tipped his head at the outburst. "It's still missing. It's the most damning piece of evidence and suggests the thief is also the murderer. The killer probably took the blessed thing and has destroyed it by now."

"*Flaming fiddles!* I was really hoping you had found the elusive thing," sighed Ophelia.

"Perhaps you can help us with another question," said Imogen. "Was the little gem we found a stone from the dagger?"

Inspector Southam leaned back in his chair and adjusted the hat on his lap. "That is one question I do have the answer to. There were no missing gems on the dagger. But I can confirm the knife was from the church vault. The vicar recognized it from an inventory meeting in the vault with Mr. Saville some years ago when he first arrived as vicar. It's quite striking. As you proposed, he suspects it was stashed here to protect it from the crown during the Dissolution of the Monasteries. In fact, most of the treasures seem to date from that time."

"Saffron Weald must have been deemed a secure location." added Imogen. "Perhaps Algernon Wainwright knows more about the history." She twisted her lips. "We didn't have a notion to examine the dagger for beauty since it was sticking out of the back of Septimus."

"Indeed." His chuckle had no humor in it this time. He made circles in the air, Tiger following his every move. "I got to see it after it was cleaned up and put into evidence. It's worth a pretty penny, I don't doubt."

Ophelia had a thought. "Have you had it valued or authenticated, Inspector? Pierre Ancien is quite the expert, you know."

"Not as yet. But it's on my agenda. I'll ask Mr. Ancien if he would consider doing that for us." He shuffled his feet. "Anything else you want to share?"

"We've actually just had a nasty run in with Mildred Chumbley at the church," began Imogen. "She's like a dog with a bone over this. It's rather vulgar. However, she did confirm that Agatha is prone to 'turns', as they call it. We visited Agatha in her home the morning after the murder and she admitted to a phobia of blood. Her emotions reach a boiling point and set her heart racing—rather like a heart attack."

"I don't suppose she has a liking for Shakespeare?" He grinned, revealing the ghost of a handsome young man.

Ophelia's shoulders began to shake violently, her face reaching a red hue as she lost the power of speech. Tears coursed down her cheeks.

The inspector stiffened, not knowing whether to perform a lifesaving technique or sit tight. He glanced at Imogen with concern in his eyes.

She swatted the air with her hand. "Don't worry, Inspector. She's just laughing. She can't utter a word until it passes. And I must say, the idea of Agatha, bless her, as the *inamorata* of Septimus, does beggar belief."

"Whoo!" sighed Ophelia finally, wiping her eyes with a handkerchief pulled from her sleeve. "That caught me right where it counts, Inspector. I was in need of a little levity, and you provided it. Thank you! I feel much more cheerful."

"All in a day's work." He smiled. "I don't suppose you've had the chance to chat to any of the other suspects?"

"Not yet, but there is more to tell about Agatha. Did you know she has a horse gambling problem?" After all, they had promised not to tell the other inhabitants of the village—not the police. And it might prove pertinent to the murder.

Astonished, the inspector cried, "No! That's a turn up for the books."

"Oh, yes! That's the real reason she has no money to do the needed improvements on her house," confirmed Imogen.

"She admitted that to you?"

"No. It was clever old Tiger. He was with us and went on a hunt. He pulled a pawnbroker's receipt for fifty pounds out of its hiding place."

"Fifty pounds! Clever dog. How on earth would she raise that sum?"

"That is rather the question," said Ophelia. "She claimed to have pawned the last of her mother's jewelry, but that may be a lie. She could be our thief."

The inspector's shock transformed to concern. "Did you confront her?"

"Her excuse was plausible, and we had no proof it was a lie, so we decided to come home and put on our thinking caps. Plus, Agatha appears unaware that Septimus had noticed the missing items and hired us to look into it."

Imogen took over. "It might be a good idea to ask around to see if Agatha was seen at the church earlier on the evening of the murder. After all, she was not on your list of people with a solid alibi. And I would think a visit to the pawn shops in Parkford might be valuable to confirm or disprove her claim."

The inspector scribbled down her suggestions.

"We tried to question Douglas but he's still extremely fragile, according to his wife, Gladys. He even canceled choir practice," Imogen continued.

"The only other person we've really had a chat with is the vicar," said Ophelia. "They were good friends, it appears, and he's quite cut up about it. They used to chat over whiskey after all their church business was done. Poor chap. I don't think he has too many friends."

"I can see that," said the inspector ruefully.

"Oh, and as we said, we checked with Celina about the Shakespeare. We can also report that her handwriting does not match that of the letters, in case you were wondering."

The inspector slapped the arm of the sofa. "That reminds me. Celina has put in an offer to buy her old boss's cottage."

"Really?" the twins said together.

"On those grounds, I have put in a request to access her bank records."

"Yes, the timing does make it suspicious but...Celina?" murmured Imogen.

"I go where the evidence leads," the inspector responded.

After dinner, Imogen suggested they go back to the church to perform surveillance on the fundraising boxes, a task which had taken a back seat since the murder.

"With everything else that's happened, I'd forgotten that Simon asked us to look into that," admitted Ophelia.

"We can take Tiger for a walk to the church then hang around the churchyard for a bit. Two birds with one stone."

Malcolm, the gardener, had undertaken the training of the dog. He used meat scraps from his grandfather's butcher shop to encourage compliance and his success was astounding. In just two weeks, Tiger had gone from pulling everyone along and choking himself, to walking at their pace by their feet like a docile lamb. The scent of bacon in Imogen's pocket did not hurt either. The improved behavior had gone a long way to winning over Ophelia.

The weather had cooled, and they passed lots of villagers out enjoying the weather. The green was full of children throwing balls and launching paper boats. Even the churchyard was busy with people placing flowers on the graves of their deceased loved ones.

The twins found a seat with a good view of the doors to the church and sat in the shade of a beech tree. Many people came and went but no one entered the church. Fortunately, Tiger was content to lay at Imogen's feet and watch the children skip by.

After an hour, Ophelia became restless. "I don't think anything is going to happen."

"You're probably right."

However, as they made motions to move, Pierre appeared looking delicious, as usual. Noticing the sisters on the bench, he ambled over.

Kissing them on the cheeks, Imogen felt that irrational urge to giggle.

"You two are the treasure at the end of the rainbow," he teased. "I was walking off my dinner and was about to turn around. I'm so glad I didn't."

They all settled back onto the bench and Tiger sniffed Pierre's hands.

"Inspector Southam will be calling you," Ophelia told him. "He needs the murder weapon to be valued."

"Do you know, ever since this 'appened, I've been meaning to talk to Bartholomew about going through all the artifacts and evaluating them. I'm going to strongly suggest they get a better lock on that vault."

"Good idea. I was able to easily spring the lock with a screwdriver."

Pierre gave Ophelia such a look. Admiration wrapped in respect. Imogen again had the feeling that the pair knew each other better than they let on. She was about to mention it when a boy of about twelve looked behind him then opened the door to the church and slipped inside.

"Can you hold Tiger for a minute?" she asked Ophelia, handing over the lead and giving her sister a pointed look.

Tiger tried to follow, but Pierre commanded him to sit.

Pulling gently, Imogen opened the church door just enough to inch through. Creeping behind a pillar she kept her eye on the boy who was walking along the left side of the church.

He stopped and checked behind him again before reaching up for the Sunday School outing box. Twiddling with it for a minute, he reached inside, pulled something out and stuffed it in his pocket.

Chapter 17

Without so much as batting an eye, Imogen pursued the boy. Ophelia and Pierre were still chatting, but a subtle glance told her that Ophelia had seen her leaving, though she gave Pierre no indication of the fact.

The youngster was skipping, almost running, and Imogen had to canter to keep up. At one point, he spun around. She stopped short, feigning interest in a flower on the hedgerow. He watched her for a moment then carried on and she was forced to observe his movements out of the corner of her eye. He was headed in the direction of the cottages on the edge of the green.

Stepping leisurely, as though she were on a casual walk through the village, Imogen followed, heart hammering against her ribs, hoping she would not miss which of the houses he entered.

Rather than walk by the cottages, she made for the pond, looking nonchalantly over her shoulder, wishing she had worn a more free flowing dress. She was just in time to catch sight of him tripping through a blue door.

Switching directions, she marched toward the *Dog and Whistle*. On this Sunday evening, the place was half filled, a merry buzz indicating gathered friends. Imogen strolled straight up to the bar.

"Evening Desmond."

His mustache wiggled as he pulled a pint. "Evening, Mrs. Pettigrew."

"I think you can call me Imogen now we sing in the choir together, Desmond."

He nodded, lips clamped in a practiced smile. "What can I get you?" He handed the expertly filled glass to a waiting customer.

"Actually, I was wondering if you know who lives in the row cottage with the bright blue door."

He lifted his chin. "That would be Jenny Taylor. Widow with five littl'uns. Broke her ankle three weeks ago. She cleans for people so that's put paid to that." He lowered his voice. "I think they're struggling." He tipped his head to a box on the counter. "We've got a collection going for her."

"Is that so?" Imogen searched in her handbag for her coin purse and dropped a handful in the box. "Thank you for the information, Desmond."

♪♪

The strains of happy chatter caused Imogen to hide behind a tree and observe her sister and Pierre. Sitting on opposite ends of the bench, each with an arm stretched along the back, only an inch separated their fingers. Relaxed, Ophelia's head hung back a little, a girlish sparkle in blue gray eyes that held Pierre's with little effort. He returned her gaze with a soft expression, holding far more meaning than a mere acquaintance deserved, his handsome features relaxed into something approaching joy. Though Imogen could not hear the words they spoke, it was obvious this was no idle small talk. If a dry twig were to fall from the old tree, Imogen was sure it would ignite like a Catherine Wheel.

Loathed to interrupt, she waited. Her news could wait.

But Tiger couldn't.

Spotting her, he sprung up, running over, causing the pair to look her way.

The magic moment burst like detergent bubbles.

"What a lovely evening," she commented as she approached. "If you want to stay Ophelia, I can take Tiger home."

"I would be honored to accompany you both back to Badger's Hollow," said Pierre, standing and sweeping off his hat like a chevalier. He gave Tiger's lead to Imogen and offered his arm to Ophelia.

"I would like that very much," she replied in a voice a shade deeper than usual.

♪♪

Once Pierre bid them farewell and they were settled in the sitting room with some tea, Ophelia asked, "And what did you discover in the church, ducky?"

Her body sagged. "That scruffy boy is the Sunday School Outing Fund thief."

Ophelia raised a brow. "But…I can tell from your tone there's more to the story."

Imogen related how she had followed him to the row of workers' cottages, then asked Desmond Ale for information on the family.

"They need the money, lovey. They probably don't have enough for food. His theft is a matter of survival. His mother may not even know where he gets the money and doesn't ask."

"This sounds exactly like something the W.I. and church should sponsor," said Ophelia clapping her hands. "It's only surprising that no one has put two and two together already."

"It's probably the distraction of the murder." Imogen pushed to her feet. "I'm going to contact the deacon. He can set a charitable effort in motion." Tiger lifted his head, swiveling his ears.

The telephone sat on a small table at the bottom of the stairs. Imogen remembered when her father had it installed. Her mother had regarded the instrument as some kind of witchcraft at first. But as soon as she realized she could talk to her grandchildren on the contraption, she was all in.

However, Simon Purchase, the deacon, apparently did not own a telephone. Imogen called the vicar to get his address instead and made plans to visit him the following morning.

♫

They were surprised to find that Simon's cottage was in the same row as the boy who had stolen the money.

"Come in, Mrs. Pettigrew. Miss Harrington." The deacon's ruddy cheeks filled into a genuine smile.

The scent of baby nappies and stale milk hit their noses as they followed Simon into a small parlor, where his wife sat holding a tiny baby over her shoulder and a toddler on her knee, her pretty face, foggy with fatigue.

Still in his blue and white striped apron, Simon lifted the garment over his head as he said, "I just got back from my rounds. I have a couple of bottles left if you'd like some?"

"Not for me thanks," said Ophelia.

"I'd love some fresh milk," responded Imogen.

He disappeared and returned with a glass before lighting up a cigarette with a match. "Lost my lighter somewhere," he explained. "Now, what can I do for you ladies?"

Imogen looked at him then at his wife, with a question on her brow.

"Oh, Sheila already knows about the thief, don't you love?"

Sheila nodded as the little boy on her lap stared wide eyed at the two identical visitors.

"We've come here to report that we have discovered who the culprit is, but we're sure that you will not want to prosecute." Imogen repeated the story.

"Well, now I just feel awful," he sighed. "We've been so busy with the new baby and all that, I haven't been paying attention to my neighbors as I should."

"You do take them any leftover milk, Simon," said his wife, her weary voice as sweet as a summer's day.

"But I'm the deacon," he sputtered. "It's my job to look out for the temporal needs of the good people of Saffron Weald." He hung his head in his hands.

"You're not alone in that duty," said Ophelia in his defense. "There's the vicar too. Sometimes things are bound to slip through the cracks. Perhaps this is the Lord's way of bringing their plight to your attention while you're so busy with your own expanding family."

"Do you think so?" He was seeking absolution.

"I do," she replied. "Now, what are we going to do about it?"

♪♪

Leaving the deacon's home, Imogen whispered. "Oh, dear! Simon smokes *and* has lost his lighter!"

"But didn't you notice how shabby their house was? I'm sure he wouldn't be able to afford an engraved, silver lighter."

"He would if he is also the thief of the items from the vault." Imogen rubbed her arm. "Oh, I really don't want it to be him. He's such a nice man with a lovely little family and deacon's serve because they feel called, not for remuneration."

They walked to the end of the street. "I feel sure it's not him," declared Ophelia. Besides, why would he involve us if *he* was the other thief?"

Imogen's shoulders drooped with relief. "Good point, lovey. Which way shall we go now?"

"My sweet tooth is bothering me," replied Ophelia. "I think we should satisfy it, don't you?"

They walked across to the high street and entered the *Jolly Lolly*. Fred Fudgeford was in the shop front today, opening boxes and re-filling the tall, glass sweet cannisters.

"Laaadies! Heeello." His pale, round face, smudged with dark shadows under the eyes, was reminiscent of a panda bear. "What can I get for you?" He dropped the box he was holding onto the counter, brows raised with expectation.

"I'll take some aniseed balls and pear drops, please," said Ophelia.

"Faaaaabulous choice!" Fred poured the hard sweets into his sparkling scales while chatting about the weather. As he handed Ophelia the bags, Arabella pushed through from the back, a frown on her face and a cigarette in her hand.

"I didn't know you smoked," said Imogen with surprise.

"It's only recent. I've had a chesty cough. The doctor thought smoking might help, but honestly, it makes me cough even more. Still, the ads seem to suggest it can help so I try to smoke one cigarette a day." She winked through the smoke. "One thing it *does* do is settle my nerves."

"How about youuuuu, Mrs. Pettigrew?" asked Fred with the signature emphasis on his vowels.

"A quarter pound of lemon sherberts, please."

"Do you suffer with your nerves?" asked Ophelia popping a hard aniseed ball into her mouth.

"Not as a rule, but the sight of Douglas with his hands covered in blood..." She shuddered. "I came home and went straight for a cigarette. Calmed me right down."

The Fudgefords were recent additions to the village having bought the confectioners after the former owner retired. "I don't mind telling you, what with the murder back in June, I'm beginning to wonder if we made the right decision moving here." She tapped the end of the cigarette into a little glass ashtray.

Shorter than his wife by a good five inches, Fred raised up on his toes and patted her arm. "Come now, sweeeeetheart. You looooove it here."

She dismissed him with her hand. "Correction. I *did* love it here. Now, I'm worried about my children all the time."

"This may not help, but it's not like a random lunatic is coming into the village and killing people willy nilly," said Ophelia through the sweet tucked into her cheek. "The murderers are killing to fix a problem."

Arabella's jaw swung from left to right. "You're right—not really helping. What if my family become the problem to fix?" She took a long drag on the cigarette then dissolved into a coughing fit.

Fred scratched his neck. "It would help if we could put the killer behind bars as soon as possible." He leaned an elbow on the counter as if he were a bartender. "I don't suppose you two are looking into it after that fine job finding the killer back in June?"

Chapter 18

Remembering that they were in need of stamps, and that they had yet to really question Patricia Snodgrass, the post mistress, the sisters continued along the high street. The post office was at a little distance from the other shops having originally been a blacksmith. When the need for horseshoes plummeted due to the popularity and accessibility of the relatively inexpensive bicycle and the coming of the train, Saffron Weald's smithy decided to sell his property and retire to the coast. Seen as a status symbol for a smallish village, the villagers petitioned his majesty's government for a post office since the closest one was in the county seat of Parkford. The postal service arrived in 1888 to great fanfare.

Patricia Snodgrass's father had been the postmaster until his death and since Patricia had never married and knew the trade inside and out, having been born in the post office, the government endowed her with the singular privilege of becoming the new postmistress. If the men gathered at the pub, the post office was often a gathering spot for the women.

The transformation of the building itself had been a topic of hot debate in 1888. Could it retain its barnlike aspect, or should it conform to the wattle and daub Elizabethan architecture of the rest of the village? Arguments were made on both sides, as were sworn enemies because of it. The result was the characteristic black and white on the façade with the old stone walls on the sides and rear. The soaring roof of the barn was converted to provide an apartment for the postmaster.

One compromise was the windows. Instead of the small diamond shaped, lead sided panes of the reign of Elizabeth, the windows were single pane, shaped like the arches of a cloister, framed with jet black timbers.

"How can I help you?" Proudly displayed behind Patricia were the rare stamps she collected, mounted in custom frames. As an enthusiastic philatelist, she loved to educate people on the origin of her latest find—whether they wanted to hear it or not.

Patricia was efficiency personified.

"I need three, second class stamps and one, first class," said Imogen, removing the letters she had written and placing them on the counter.

Patricia smiled through round, black-rimmed glasses and opened her leatherbound book of official stamps. "How are you both enjoying the choir?"

"Other than someone being murdered while we were singing, you mean," retorted Ophelia.

Patricia stopped searching and raised both hands to her waist. "Ah, silly me! What was I thinking. That did put a damper on things." She squinted one eye before returning to her task.

"How long have you been in the choir?" asked Imogen.

"Years," Patricia replied while painstakingly tearing the stamps carefully from the sheet, one by one.

"Did you join before or after Agatha? You're cousins, aren't you?"

Patricia stopped, pulling her bottom lip over her teeth in a most unbecoming expression of aversion. "We are loosely related, yes." Handing Imogen the stamps she continued. "I joined first having lived here without moving away. Agatha left to study at Whitelands College in Roehampton for her teacher training course."

Imogen decided to take a chance and play dumb. "I can't help noticing the animosity between you two. Has there been a falling out?"

Patricia stretched her neck on one side as though gathering her patience. "As I told your sister, it's a rather long and sordid story, I'm afraid."

Imogen put a finger to the corner of her mouth and lied, "Oh, she didn't tell me. We aren't pressed for time—if you feel comfortable telling me, that is."

With no other customers to eavesdrop, the post mistress recounted a similar tale to the one she had shared with Ophelia the day of the murder. "I am strongly of the opinion that a person's last wishes should be honored. If my great-great-grandfather wanted his oldest son to receive the inheritance, that was his prerogative and should be respected by his descendants. He was under no obligation to divvy out the wealth to his brothers. Besides, it would have meant selling the farm which was something he wanted to avoid at all costs. It's just too bad he didn't get round to writing it down in an official will."

"And Agatha is still bitter about it?" asked Imogen.

Patricia's lips were pressed so tight, an oiled flea could not have passed through them. "Can you believe she had the temerity to ask me for money to fix her roof. Do I look like I have that kind of money?" She gestured around the post office.

"Considering the feud, it must have been difficult for Agatha to make the request," said Ophelia, playing devil's advocate.

Patricia exhaled with exaggeration. "The irony is that all the money is long gone—but I'm not about to tell *her* that."

"Gone?" exclaimed Imogen.

"The land tax and death duties kept syphoning money away. There was precious little cash handed down and my great-grandfather, the heir to the land, was forced to sell a large chunk of it to pay those taxes. Then repairs were needed on broken fences and the like, and it all frizzled away by the time my grandfather died. Why do you think my father took the job of postmaster? It was to keep a roof over his head."

"Why haven't you told this to Agatha?"

Patricia grated her square jaw. "Pride I suppose. Look, I do alright, but I certainly don't have enough to pay for her roof. Agatha seems to think I'm sitting on bags of gold coins and that's just not the case."

"I see," said Imogen, looking down at an impressive collection of metal wax stamps under the glass countertop. "What a lovely assortment of seals you have."

"Thank you!" Her tone revealed she was grateful to have moved on from the sensitive topic of the inheritance. "It takes a lot of effort but I search for them at estate sales and antique shops. Pierre helped me find these two." She pointed to one of brass and one made of ivory.

"We're so fortunate we can merely purchase a stamp to stick on our letter in these modern times, but these are a work of art."

"Indeed," replied Patricia. "How awful it must have been for ordinary folk not to receive letters."

Imogen traced her finger across the glass. "Didn't one have to pay a courier before stamps?"

Patricia nodded, grabbing a duster to wipe the fingerprints Imogen had left on the glass. "Upon receipt. Only the wealthy could afford it."

"Do you think Shakespeare was wealthy enough?" It was a rather clumsy effort to introduce the topic.

Ophelia frowned.

"I suppose so," replied Patricia. "Especially after he became so famous."

"Do you enjoy his works?" Imogen ploughed on, still staring at the old-fashioned stamps.

"Uh—not particularly. Had to read some at school, of course, but it's not something I would read for leisure. I prefer Austen."

♪♪

As they walked home, Ophelia teasing her sister about the ham-fisted way she had brought up the Bard, they bumped into the colonel coming out of the *Golden Crust* bakery. Ophelia offered him her bag of sweets.

He put up a hand in protest. "No, thank you. I don't indulge."

Imogen briefly thought how terrible life would be without the odd sweetie.

"Did you hear the funeral will be on Thursday?" he said in his clipped tone. "The vicar wants the choir to sing."

"Seems fitting since Septimus enjoyed listening to us so much. Do you know which hymn it will be?" asked Imogen.

"Douglas mentioned *'How Great is God in Heaven Above'*. Apparently, it was Septimus's favorite."

"Oh. I don't know that one," said Imogen with some anxiety.

"If I can get a copy of the music, we can practice at home," Ophelia assured her.

"It's not too hard," said the colonel. He swung his head from side to side and dropped his voice. "Don't suppose you know any more about the investigation?"

Even though they did not consider the colonel a suspect since he had an alibi, they had not actually made much progress they felt comfortable sharing.

"It's moving rather slowly, as far as we know," she replied. "On that topic, I don't suppose you know anyone who has a passion for Shakespeare?"

He rubbed the skin behind his ears. "My wife loved it. Dragged me to every blessed play she could find."

"I was thinking more of someone who lives here in the village—perhaps a woman?"

The colonel's eyes bulged with comprehension. "Ah! Is that a clue?" He pursed his lips. "The vicar's wife has a bit of a thing for it. Keeps suggesting the drama society do one of his comedies. I keep voting it down."

"Anyone else?" asked Imogen, secretly scandalized at the thought that Septimus's love interest could be a married woman. And the vicar's wife, at that!

The colonel snapped his fingers. "Agatha. She was going on and on about Shakespeare at choir practice at the beginning of summer."

Imogen and Ophelia locked incredulous eyes.

Chapter 19

It was more difficult to get rid of the colonel than the twins anticipated as he continued to probe, asking if they knew of any possible motives and other crime related topics. Eventually, the vagueness of their comments clued him in, and he bid them goodbye.

Here was a fact the sisters could not deny or ignore—Agatha loved Shakespeare.

"However absurd it may seem, Agatha must now be the top candidate for Septimus's beloved," declared Ophelia.

"I know! It beggars belief. *But* it would explain the beauty of the handwriting—as a former teacher, she would have instructed her students on the finer mechanics of perfect penmanship day in and day out," added Imogen. "We need to find an example of her writing."

"Yes. There is nothing for it but to confront her," announced Ophelia.

"Absolutely!" agreed Imogen.

When Agatha answered her door, she was even more unkempt than the last time they had called. She had been noticeably absent from church and today, had still not made it out of the unflattering nightdress. Purple shadows under bloodshot eyes betrayed serious lack of sleep, and her matted hair suggested excessive restlessness in bed. Tear stains on her cheeks telegraphed a type of grief that was stronger than mere shock at being present at an acquaintance's murder.

"Uh, I'm not really up for visitors today," she croaked as Ophelia and Imogen pushed past her into a pungent cloud of musky odor.

"It is imperative that we speak to you," replied Ophelia, heading straight for the kitchen. A quick glance betrayed total disarray in the little parlor.

Dirty pans piled high in the kitchen sink and used plates and glasses scattered over the table were further evidence of a woman experiencing unbridled misery. Imogen flung open the kitchen window, rolled up her sleeves and began to clear the table. She filled the old kettle to heat water for washing up the pans and plates.

A defeated Agatha sank into a chair, her flabby face flopping into her hands.

"We know about the love letters," said Ophelia, deciding to get straight to the point rather than beat about the bush when the woman was so obviously in great pain.

Agatha's head snapped up, her red eyes wary. "What love letters?"

Ophelia reached out a hand and touched Agatha's elbow. "Look, there's no need to dissemble with us, Agatha. We know that you and Septimus were sweethearts."

The lined, anguished face fell apart. Great sobs racked her large frame. The sister's gazes met in mutual agreement that they would wait for the worst of the emotional storm to pass.

Eventually, the thunder reduced to a distant rumble.

"Why don't you tell us the whole story?" encouraged Ophelia gently.

Agatha pulled out a well-used handkerchief and blew the roof off. Imogen pursed her lips to prevent an ill-timed peal of laughter.

Wiping her eyes, Agatha began. "About eight months ago, members of the choir were chatting. Septimus was at most of our practices and joined in the conversation. Though he was tone deaf, he appreciated listening to the music of others. The talk wandered to literature. I had stumbled onto Shakespeare at teacher training college and was smitten. I'm a romantic at heart." She dabbed her prominent nose. "So, I mentioned it. I was stunned when everyone shot the notion of his genius down saying Shakespeare's manners of speech were outdated and above the average fellow's ability to understand. Even the colonel didn't defend him.

"Then wonderful Septimus piped up in my defense, a veritable knight in shining armor. He admitted no experience with Shakespeare's work but supported my right to an opinion on the matter. I can't tell you how grateful I was amid the clatter of dissenters."

The noise of dishes from the sink temporarily derailed Agatha's narration. "You don't have to do that, Imogen."

"I know, but an ordered house promotes an ordered mind. I'm happy to help. Keep going with your story. I confess, I'm fascinated."

Agatha brought the tips of her fingers together. "Whenever we had choir practice after that, I was sure Septimus was glancing at me when he thought I wasn't looking. And it seemed that he went out of his way to speak to me and accompany me to the church door."

Of course, she could have been right, but Ophelia feared that Agatha saw what she wanted to see and that Septimus's behavior had not actually changed, only Agatha's perception of it.

"We were about the same age, he and I, and I have not known much of tenderness or affection in my life. Cupid's arrow sunk deep." She fiddled with the handkerchief. "Unbecoming as it is for a woman to initiate a relationship, I decided to take a page out of the Bard's play *As You Like It* and write an anonymous letter confessing my love." Her cheeks flushed crimson and she looked up with sheepish eyes. "I daresay you think I'm an old fool."

"On the contrary," Ophelia assured her. "Who are we to judge the heart of another?"

So, it was Septimus who had not known the identity of his admirer, not the other way round as they had surmised.

Imogen finished the pans and came to sit with eager eyes. "Go on."

"Orlando hung secret letters on trees in the forest which hardly seemed practical for the churchyard of Saffron Weald." A slight smile cracked her wide mouth. "I decided to place the letter in the pocket of his Sunday robes."

"Brilliant," whispered Imogen, her countenance shining bright with reflected excitement.

Agatha's expression drooped. "But I heard nothing. I tried to read his face at the next choir practice, but he was a closed book. It seemed I had aimed my shot and failed miserably. But I reasoned that I had invested little of my affections at that point.

I shelved the incident, filing it under life experience. Why was I thinking an old spinster like me could find love?"

Imogen flashed a peek at her sister's face. It was filled with something approaching pity and her heart cracked open. Ophelia's spinsterhood was not a topic they broached, but Imogen had always felt for a sister who did not know the bliss of a loving companion or the joy of children.

"Three weeks later, I arrived early at choir practice. As I arranged myself in my seat, I glimpsed the corner of something sticking out of one of the hymnals in front of me. My heart leapt when I saw that it was a missive. It was addressed to no one, but *I* knew! People had begun to arrive so I slipped the love note into my handbag so that I could relish it in private at home."

A well-formed image of Cyrano de Bergerac flashed into Ophelia's mind as comprehension dawned. After picturing the lineup of the choir, she quickly realized that Celina stood right next to Agatha in the choir stalls.

Septimus thought his secret admirer was Celina!

Imogen was staring at her with a query. Ophelia shrugged. The man was dead. What harm was there in letting a lonely woman believe *she* was the object of Septimus's affections?

Head bowed, the headmistress had missed the silent exchange between the sisters.

"I cannot readily express how the letter affected me. Words are insufficient to do the heavenly emotion justice. Unlike me, Septimus had gone to the trouble of extracting relevant lines from Shakespeare's works and compiling them into love letters. My heart was aflutter." Her countenance took on a celestial mien amidst the purple bags. She clutched clenched fists to her ample chest. "To find love at my age!" Agatha looked to Ophelia for confirmation and Imogen's soul flooded with sympathy.

Ophelia merely nodded though her eyes slumped a little at the corners.

"And so began our love affair. We traded notes secretly the whole summer until—" She broke down. "The secrecy added another dimension, you know." Her voice was fractured, her dull eyes watery. "No one had any idea and yet our feelings were so vast they filled the whole sanctuary. No! The whole world. It was the best feeling I've ever experienced."

For Ophelia, the joyful story had morphed into a tragedy on more than one level.

"When Douglas staggered out, hands covered in blood, my phobia kicked in and my heart began to race. I couldn't catch my breath. But when Douglas uttered Septimus's name, my world buckled completely. I blacked out. I didn't want to be revived. I wanted to join him in death.

"I don't know how I got home, but someone brought me and tucked me into bed. The doctor had given me a sedative for the shock." She looked up, her eyelashes glistening with captured tears. "But there is no medicine for a broken heart."

Her final words cracked on delivery and Imogen felt a stinging behind her own eyes.

"So, I will go on as before…but changed forever. I now know what it is to be loved by the most decent of men. I shall treasure that memory until the day I die."

Chapter 20

Walking down the path of Agatha's frayed cottage, Imogen just couldn't keep her thoughts to herself. In a tight whisper she declared, "There is no way Agatha could have killed Septimus. She was in *love* with him."

Ophelia stopped. "You're thinking with your heart, ducky. I would say she's moved to the top of the suspect list for me."

"What? No! Why?"

Ophelia indicated the house as a lace curtain twitched, and put a finger to her lips. "Let's move out of range."

Once they were a little down the road, Ophelia continued, "Are you familiar with the story of Cyrano?"

"Of course. It's about a quiet, unassuming man who writes love letters for an illiterate, handsome devil who can't put two words together, to help him woo the girl he loves. What does that have to do with this?"

"Who sits next to Agatha in the choir?" Ophelia asked.

Imogen halted and closed her eyes. "Uh…oh!" Her eyes tore open. "You're saying that Septimus thought the letters were from Celina?"

"It makes more sense to me. Septimus was not a traditionally handsome fellow but he did have a few things going for him. And he was a quiet, contemplative chap. Do you really see him being attracted to pushy, overbearing Agatha?"

Chewing her cheek as she pondered, Imogen had to agree. "Oh. How sad."

A young mother with two children passed them and Ophelia dropped her voice to a whisper. "Since the parties had not yet approached each other in the open, I think it's a pretty safe bet to assume that Septimus believed his admirer was Celina. Since the letter he received had been placed secretly in his robes, he replied in kind, placing his letter in a hymn book where he knew Celina sat. But Agatha found it by mistake and naturally assumed it was a reply to her own love letter."

"A comedy of errors," murmured Imogen.

"It happens quite often—it's happened to me more than once. You catch someone looking at you, so you think they're interested, especially if you've had your eye on them, but really they're considering what they want to cook for dinner and you just happened to move into their line of sight."

"I think Septimus believed the letter was from Celina because he already admired her. She's a pretty, conservative librarian. Much more his taste. He must have been terribly flattered to think his feelings were reciprocated."

They passed by the pub and made for the green.

Imogen took up the theory. "So, he would take his time getting his response just right. Plus, getting books out of the library would give him the opportunity to signal to Celina that he had found her letter and was crafting his reply. He must have thought he was sending her all sorts of hints but she never saw them for what they were because she had *not* sent the original letter."

"Exactly! The mind plays tricks when we think someone is romantically interested in us."

Imogen stopped again, hand on her hip. "Ok, out with it. You're much too familiar with this predicament."

"What? It's never happened to you?"

"I didn't say that…" Imogen chortled.

Crossing the bridge over the pond Ophelia said, "There may have been a conductor I once had a crush on. Silver, longish hair, sharp chin and very athletic figure. I was convinced he kept looking at me but it turned out he was actually eyeing the young viola player *behind* me. Since I thought he was interested, I invited him to go out for a drink, which was incredibly gutsy and progressive of me back then. He graciously accepted but spent the whole evening talking about the viola player, asking if I thought he was too old to make a play for her. I can't tell you how humiliating it was. I felt like a complete fool. They ended up getting married. Your turn."

They were down the other side of the bridge and headed for home.

"It was in primary school," began Imogen. "Matthew Greer asked me to meet him at lunchtime. You probably don't remember him, but I'd held a candle for him all year and was absolutely over the moon. When I found him outside, he asked me to help with his English homework. I was devastated. He was only interested in my brain."

"Did you help him?"

"I certainly did not!" retorted Imogen.

They had reached the top of their road and could see Badger's Hollow.

"Do you see where I'm going with this now?" asked Ophelia. "If Agatha somehow found out that Septimus believed *Celina* was his admirer—like I did when I went out with the conductor, well, hell hath no fury like a woman scorned and all that."

"Let me think it through," said Imogen, waving to Arabella Fudgeford who was on the other side of the street with her children. "A furious, slighted Agatha arrives early for choir. She hides in the crypt where she awaits an unsuspecting Septimus. When he opens the vault, she follows then stabs him in the back." Imogen frowned. "What about her blood phobia?"

"If she leaves fast enough, she can disappear before the blood appears," responded Ophelia.

"Alright. She nips up and out the back of the church, staying hidden until several more choir members arrive. When Douglas appears covered with blood, she can lean into her phobia providing herself with a solid alibi."

Ophelia took over. "Well done! If *she* can't have him, no one can."

"But why would she choose stabbing? Wouldn't poison be a better choice for someone with a fear of blood?" asked Imogen, reaching for the latch on the gate.

With pouty lips, Ophelia considered the conundrum. "Perhaps Agatha is the thief too and we were wrong about the premeditation. If Septimus found her in the vault she would have acted on impulse, grabbing whatever was close. Her anger about him liking Celina would fuel her fury. She *is* in desperate need of funds and Patricia has no inclination or money to help her."

"Pawning church artifacts is a far better explanation for the receipt for £50, but somehow it still doesn't feel right to me," said Imogen.

She put her key in the door and Tiger leapt out, full of repressed energy and excitement to see them. "Down boy," she said, ruffling his fur.

"I know what you mean," agreed Ophelia, sliding past the doting pair. "I feel unsettled too. How can such a pillar of the community be a chronic gambler, a thief *and* a murderer?"

"I'd forgotten about the gambling problem. We need to ask the inspector if he's had any luck investigating the pawnshops."

"Or we could go ourselves," suggested Ophelia. "I did notice the name on the pawnshop receipt—*Humble Henry's Hock*. I think we deserve a day out. How about tomorrow since Malcolm is coming to do the garden?"

♪♪

"You sure this is the place?" asked the crusty cab driver, peering out of the windscreen. "Couple'a nice ladies like you? Don't seem quite right."

"This is the name we were given," said Ophelia, in a desperate tone that put all her drama skills to the test. "We're in dire need of funds, you see."

The taxi driver shook his head.

Parkford was a respectable town, but even respectable towns hide a seedy section. *Humble Henry's Hock* was slapdab in the middle of it. Rubbish blew along the curb of narrow streets housing a dusty, hodgepodge of architecture. Persons of ill repute slunk around or loitered in doorways.

Imogen agreed with the cab driver.

Ophelia handed him the fare and stepped out, while Imogen hovered close to her side.

"Don't worry. I know a move or two if anyone tries anything," declared Ophelia.

"How in the world…?"

"Do you think I stayed home alone waiting for prince charming to arrive, because I was single? Heavens no! There was a whole wide world waiting for me and I was darned if I was going to miss it. But I had to learn to take care of myself."

Lips slammed together in a thin line, Imogen gripped her sister's arm as they looked up at the seedy pawnshop with its peeling, black paint and grimy windows.

"Just follow my lead," commanded Ophelia.

The tall buildings on either side of the narrow street limited the amount of sun that could penetrate but it seemed bright compared to the inside of the smelly shop. After several seconds of adjustment, Imogen jumped out of her skin as the hulking silhouette of the pawnbroker broke through the dingy gloom. His weepy eyes hurried between the two identical women.

Rubbing together rough hands clad in fingerless gloves, he wheezed, "'Ow can I 'elp you today?"

Expensive jewelry had never appealed to Ophelia who always said she would rather use the money for travel. Imogen, on the other hand, possessed a few quality pieces, some of which her husband had bought for her on anniversaries and birthdays. However, especially since her husband's death, they all carried sentimental value far in excess of how much they were worth, and Ophelia had to bring all her powers of persuasion to bear to convince her sister to offer them up to the pawnbrokers. She had emphasized that it was all in a good cause and vowed that they would repossess the intrinsic items as soon as the investigation was over, and well within the thirty-day contract.

Ophelia withdrew a single grey pearl on a silver chain and placed it on the grubby glass countertop.

Broken nails lined with dirt, reached forward to pick up the treasure with surprising reverence. The frightening man held the pearl to his bulbous, purple nose and sniffed as if holding a rose rather than a necklace, then snatched a magnifier from the pocket of his sagging jacket and pinched it between the top and bottom of his eye socket.

Imogen trembled as his cracked lips spread into a counterfeit smile, revealing blackened, chipped teeth.

"Nice. Very nice." He spoke just how one would imagine Fagin's voice to be. Peering up, the magnifier still clamped in place, his pupil appeared grotesquely oversized.

Imogen squeaked.

"Twenty quid."

Now Imogen squawked with indignation—the pearl was worth twice that. Sensing her consternation, Ophelia placed a quieting hand on her sister's arm.

Ophelia's blue gray eyes crinkled but no one would describe the action as a smile. She held out her palm for the jewel. "I am disappointed. I was told you were an honest man. I will accept nothing less than £40."

The greasy man pulled the gem closer to his chest, flicking his head. "Thirty."

Ophelia's hand was still outstretched, her gaze steely. Imogen felt a certain pride.

Henry grasped a strand of stringy, long hair that fell from the sides of his black hat, framing a face reminiscent of a gnarled tree trunk, full of deep grooves and knots. "Thirty-two."

"I have told you my terms," barked Ophelia.

He moved a dishonest arm as if to place the jewel in her hand. "Thirty-five. Final offer."

"Thirty-eight."

Spitting dark liquid into a filthy pail on the counter, he cried, "Done!" scaring Imogen half to death.

Soiled fingers reached for the cash register. He pressed a lever and removed the pound notes.

"I'll need a receipt," said Ophelia, watching his every move like a hawk. Imogen had never seen this side of her sister. "Write it out to Miss Swithers, please."

Henry pulled out a pad of paper with the shop's name embossed at the top and began to scrawl. "Who told you 'bout me?"

Having now met the crooked proprietor and seen the dismal place, Ophelia was absolutely sure Agatha would not have given her real name. In fact, she was more than a little surprised that the proper headmistress had done business with Henry at all.

"A friend. In her late forties with curly, honeyish hair and a small, brown birth mark on her neck just here." She pointed to the dip where her clavicle bones met.

Henry cracked his vast knuckles. "Oh, yeah. I 'member 'er."

Ophelia's breath caught in her throat. "She needed to offload a silver platter, I think."

"Nah!" His dirty finger pointed through the glass to a hideous necklace with small diamonds set in heavy gold. "That's 'ers."

"My mistake." Ophelia's mind raced, searching for a question to further the conversation while she processed her disappointment. "I wonder, has she ever sold any other items to you?" She hoped such a question would not be considered inappropriate in the world of pawn.

"A ring. That's all."

Flaming fiddles!

He swiped his nose with the back of his gloved hand. "You interested?"

"I-I thought perhaps I could buy something back for her." Ophelia dropped her eyes to the floor. "But it's all a little expensive."

She reached for the proffered receipt.

"You ever wanna sell that," said the giant, pointing to Imogen's gold locket. "You know where to find me."

Imogen instinctively reached up to protect the beloved necklace with her hand, as if his words had the power to wind themselves around the chain and pull it from her neck.

"Good day," said Ophelia, bustling her traumatized sister out of the door.

Chapter 21

Safely out on the pavement, Imogen sucked in a huge breath of fresh air mingled with relief, praising heaven that they had survived the ordeal.

Ophelia, on the other hand, was grinning from ear to ear. "Well, wasn't that fun!"

"Fun!" cried Imogen in horror. "You need your head examined! I think old Henry dines on small children. Whatever would possess Agatha to lower her standards to that degree?"

Ophelia inhaled. "Desperation."

"I can categorically state that Agatha was taking an unnecessary risk coming here. But at least we know she *was* telling the truth. She did pawn *jewelry* and not stolen goods from the church vault." Her anxious fingers were still gripping the locket.

"So how did Agatha obtain the knife, if she killed Septimus?"

As a man in a dirty mackintosh brushed past them, they speedily tottered out of the dark alley of a street and onto a proper road. Imogen wondered if this was what it felt like to be released from prison.

"Yes. That does put a dent in our theory. Looks like we need to broaden our investigation. Since we're here, I suggest we find a tea shop and ask the staff about other pawnshops in the area to see if we can find any religious artifacts for sale. Even after Henry's disappointing revelation, I scanned that place but didn't see anything that looked like it came from our church."

"I was too busy praying for my life," yelped Imogen. "And I've clearly led a far more sheltered life than you, but I don't think items known or suspected to be stolen would be displayed anyway, lovey. I'm sure those transactions are backroom deals."

"You're probably right, but since we're here, I'd like to check."

They wandered through a tangle of unknown streets until they were on more familiar ground and entered a tea shop painted a jolly orange. The stout hostess looked vaguely familiar.

"Ophelia Harrington?" The woman patted her chest. "It's Betty Phillips. Betty Farrow, as was. Fancy seeing you after all these years. I used to play the violin with you."

"Betty! Of course! How are you?" A thread of memory was pulling in Ophelia's brain.

"I used to sit about five chairs away from you in the county orchestra. You helped me hold my bow properly," Betty continued.

At this hint, the memories flooded back. In their school days, Betty had been a good-natured girl with blonde curls and a splash of freckles over a button nose. The gray-haired woman before them bore little resemblance to that girl now, but her personality was just as vibrant.

"Is this your shop?" asked Imogen.

"It's my daughter's place. I help with waitressing from time to time when someone calls in sick." She clapped her hands. "What 'till I tell Arthur who I saw today. You still look like two peas in a pod."

Arthur Phillips, Ophelia remembered. A muscular boy whose biceps strained through the white cotton of his shirts when he played the trumpet. His mesmerizing, amber eyes often caused her to lose her place in the music.

"Follow me. I'll put you at our best table."

"Are there many pawnshops in Parkford?" asked Imogen casually as Betty handed them the menu.

Betty's eyes narrowed.

"She's going to tell her husband we're hard up," thought Ophelia. *"Oh, well. I'll probably never see her again."*

"There's one on Pike Road that I wouldn't advise," Betty responded. "Then there are two more. One on Lloyd Road and one on Farmington Close. Much better class of customer."

She took their order and Imogen whispered, "Oops! I'm sorry I wasn't more subtle. I bet she thinks we need money so badly we need to pawn our possessions."

Ophelia flicked the napkin and placed it on her knee. "It was rather a clumsy way to ask, ducky. But I suppose it's a small price to pay to further our investigation."

"Back in Surrey, everyone knew we were quite well off and there were certain expectations. It's quite refreshing to be thought of as hard-up."

♪♪

The second pawnshop of the day on Farmington Road was named *The Honest Penny*. The man at this counter bore a striking resemblance to a weasel, with a narrow, pointed nose and small, active eyes.

Ophelia placed a ring on the counter. Imogen had received this piece from an old beau. The pawnbroker picked up the ring and used a similar magnifier to the one Henry had used. Imogen wandered around the store as Ophelia haggled with the man. As she had suspected, there were no religious artifacts on display here either.

Ophelia leaned on the counter. "If I had something more valuable to sell, would you be able to help me?"

The thin man's beady eyes became wary. "I don't know what you mean."

"I heard from a—" she looked over her shoulder and Imogen felt the impulse to curl up with laughter "—friend that I might be able to buy or sell *unique* pieces here."

His thin lips disappeared. "Don't know where you heard that, missus. There's a reason this place is called *The Honest Penny*. Everything here is above board."

She took the money and the receipt. "Please accept my apologies. I meant no offense. My contact must have got the wrong end of the stick."

♪♪

The third store, *Vintage Treasures*, was a blend of the two previous ones. Items hung from the ceiling and walls and the sisters had to duck under and through them. Dust and smoke in the air made Imogen sneeze. The proprietor of this establishment resembled a sloth; longish, brown hair parted in the middle, a short nose and small tired eyes that drooped. He was smoking a pipe but placed it on a wooden dish when they entered.

"Yes?" His voice grated like a rusty gate in the wind.

Ophelia withdrew their third item from her capacious handbag; an unattractive but valuable bracelet made of coins from around the world.

The sloth's drowsy eyes widened. He examined the dates on each coin. Some were over one hundred years old.

"£10."

Ophelia pulled the bracelet back. "You insult me, sir. I shall take my business elsewhere."

He raised a sinewy hand in apology. "Let's say £15 and stay friends."

"Do you think I'm a fool? One of these coins alone might bring that."

"I see I'm dealing with a lady more knowledgeable than the average person," he said, licking his lips. "Excuse me. I'll raise my bid to £25 and give you forty days to pay it back."

Ophelia raised her eyes to the right and scowled.

"She really should join the village drama society," thought Imogen.

Ophelia handed back the bracelet. "£25 will do nicely. I shall need a receipt."

"Of course." He pulled out a receipt pad and began to write.

Ophelia curved her spine and leaned forward as she watched. "If I had something much more valuable and perhaps not quite so…legitimate, would I be able to work with you?"

Imogen pretended to be browsing but every sense was on high alert.

The sleepy eyes perked up. "Not legitimate?"

"A friend of mine wanted me to ask. They've recently come into possession of something from the fifteenth century they need to leverage."

His dark eyes slid back and forth like marbles on a moving tray. "It just so happens that I'm a bit of an expert on antique artifacts. Just a couple of weeks ago, I did business with a fellow for something not unlike what you 'ave described."

"He wouldn't want this item back, you understand," Ophelia responded.

The sloth tapped the side of his nose. "I get your message loud and clear, missus." He swallowed. "However, I prefer to do that kind of business *after* hours."

Ophelia's heart skipped a beat. "Of course. Do you have a card?"

♫

"The thief is a man!" cried Imogen with excitement as they hurried back to the bus stop.

"Yes! I wonder if I should have pushed him for a description," replied Ophelia.

"I'd say you need to tread lightly with his sort. Any misstep would probably have shut him down. No, you did the right thing, Ophelia. But now we have his card. It will enable us to set up a fake buy or something. Catch him red-handed."

"You've been reading spy novels again," laughed Ophelia.

Spotting a telephone box a little further down the road, Ophelia suggested they call the inspector with their news.

"Southam!" he barked into the telephone.

"Inspector, it's Ophelia Harrington." Imogen's ear was pressed to the receiver too.

His tone improved slightly. "Got any information for me?"

"I wonder, did you question any pawnbrokers in Parkford?" she asked before dishing out the details of their investigation.

"Tried. All snapped tight as a clam when I started poking around. Suspicious by nature that lot. Wait! Have you been meddling?"

"I could lie and say no, Inspector, but then I couldn't tell you what we dug up."

A throaty rumbling noise came down the line. "Out with it then."

They told him about the owner of *Vintage Treasures* and that he had all but confessed to dealing in antique stolen goods on the black market.

"Well, well, well," said the inspector with no small hint of admiration. "And he said the person he dealt with was a man?"

"Yes. That moves us further in the right direction doesn't it, Inspector?"

"And did you verify this man was from Saffron Weald?"

Twitching trumpets! She had not! It was unlike her to be so sloppy.

"Uh, no. I'm afraid I didn't. We were skating on pretty thin ice and I didn't want to spook him. However, we did get his card and intimate that we would contact him to sell such an item."

"That's better than nothing," replied the inspector. "We can set up a phony sale and arrest the pawnbroker. During interrogation I can demand he describe the person he did dodgy business with. Well done, ladies!"

After a delicious dinner of baked liver and onions, the sisters reconvened at the kitchen table with their notebook.

"I think we need to separate the two crimes until we have proof they are actually connected," said Imogen. "We cannot simply assume that Septimus was killed because he interrupted the thief, even though he was killed with a religious relic. The murderer could have been waiting for him in the crypt for some other reason and killed him when he entered the vault."

Chin thrust forward, Ophelia grudgingly agreed. "Though I believe it is too much of a coincidence for these crimes *not* to be connected, it is probably prudent to separate them at this time."

"Which also means that although we now have evidence that the thief is male, we cannot conclusively state that the killer is the same man," pointed out Imogen.

Tiger scratched at the back door and Imogen let him out into the garden.

"Which brings us full circle back to Agatha, the slighted lover," said Ophelia, doodling next to Agatha's name.

"She certainly seems to be the top suspect for the murder. But let's consider who else it could be?"

Ophelia flicked through the pages of notes. "Clues. Since we're separating the crimes, let's first evaluate the clues we found at the scene of the thefts. First off is the drop of wax. Frankly, without a beautiful, full fingerprint embedded in it, the wax is of little use."

"Agreed," said Imogen.

"Second, the dirty cassock. A better name would be habit, I think, since it has a hood. Because of that, we know it is not one that belonged to Septimus or the vicar."

"Which reminds me, we were going to talk to Matilda to see if any of their monk's costumes are missing," said Imogen.

"Let's call tomorrow and follow up on that." Ophelia drew the pencil under the next clue. "The lighter. It seems to be quite valuable and has that pretty design. It was probably used by the thief to light the candles in the vault."

"That means the thief is likely someone who smokes. That includes Arabella, Simon, Septimus, Douglas and Desmond. Of those people, the ones that are visibly short of cash are Simon and Septimus, who both reported the stealing to us."

"Uggh. This feels like a dead end," complained Imogen.

"Don't lose hope, ducky! Let's switch to the clues from the murder." She turned to the relevant page in the notebook. "The little amber jewel. Thanks to the inspector we know that it was not dislodged from the dagger. Therefore, it is from a brooch or hair comb or some other decorative item that might be used by a woman."

A thought struck Imogen. "Or a man's tiepin. Wilf used to wear one with a ruby."

"Good thinking," responded Ophelia, scribbling it down. "Amber is not such a popular stone for jewelry. I can't think of anyone who has worn such an item, can you?"

"No. What's the next clue?" Imogen asked.

"The note in Septimus's pocket about checking the candles."

"Perhaps when we found the drop of wax, Septimus undertook an inventory of the candles to see if any were missing."

"That is a credible guess. Unfortunately, we will never know."

A short bark alerted the sisters that Tiger was ready to come back inside.

"Next up is the blue thread," continued Ophelia as Imogen refilled Tiger's water bowl.

"Everyone wears blue. It's one of the more popular colors," sighed Imogen.

Ophelia snapped her fingers. "I saw a blue scarf hanging on the coat stand in Agatha's hallway."

"I have a blue scarf. You have a blue scarf," retorted her sister. "I'm betting every female in the village owns one."

"Point taken. Next, the presence of vinegar on Septimus's sleeve."

"Now, that one is a stretch. He could have eaten something pickled that day and got some of the vinegar on his jacket."

"I still think it's worth asking Reggie who has bought his ridiculous pickled watermelon," responded Ophelia. "And finally, the missing ledger. I thought it might have appeared by now."

"I've been thinking about that," said Imogen throwing Tiger a treat. "In Scotland they use dogs in the police force to help them track suspects because they have such a highly developed sense of smell. I think we could introduce some of Septimus's clothing to Tiger and then take him round the village to visit people who do not have an alibi for the time of the murder, to see if he picks up the scent anywhere. The leather book is bound to carry Septimus's scent."

Ophelia rested her chin in her hands. "That is not a totally ludicrous plan." She glanced over at the dog. "He *should* earn his room and board. And that elusive book might be the key to the whole mystery."

The clock struck twelve. "We have a lot to do tomorrow; evaluating the dagger with Pierre, setting up the rendezvous with the sloth and taking Tiger on a fieldtrip." Ophelia pushed back her chair.

Imogen stood and Tiger lifted his nose. "Not to mention calling Matilda and asking Reggie about his watermelon."

"And it might not be a bad idea to find out if Celina knew Septimus was infatuated with her."

Slowly making their way up the stairs they were jolted when the telephone shattered the peace.

Their shoulders tightened and they cast worried glances at each other.

"It must be important at this hour. I'll go," volunteered Ophelia, but Imogen followed her down.

"Miss Harrington?" It was the inspector, his voice taut as a drum. "There's been another murder!"

Chapter 22

Ophelia raised alarmed eyes. "A murder! Who?"
Imogen slammed into her sister to listen in.
"Agatha Trumble. She's been strangled with a scarf."
Ophelia almost dropped the phone. "*Bloomin' bagpipes!*"
"She had invited the colonel over to discuss school business since he is one of the governors, but when he arrived, no one answered. He thought perhaps she had been held up somewhere so returned home to await her call. But by nine o' clock he began to worry and called Constable Hargrove. I've been at her cottage since ten o'clock. We'll have to postpone our buy with the pawnbroker as this must take priority now."
"I understand," said Ophelia, clutching the skin of her neck. "Is there any sign of why she might have been targeted?"
"Looks like she was blackmailing someone."
"Blackmail!"
"We found several pound notes clutched in her hand when she died, and my men found crumpled demand notices in the wastebin in her bedroom. Looks like she was practicing to get the wording just right. By the way, the handwriting matches the love letters we found in Septimus's cottage."
"I hope you won't be angry with us, but we recently deduced that Agatha had to be the author of the letters and confronted her. She confessed. We were going to tell you soon. The irony is that we actually think Septimus did not know it was her."
Silence at the other end betrayed his shock.
Ophelia cleared her throat and in a tentative tone asked, "Did Agatha disclose the name of the killer in her demands?"
"I've warned you about confronting possible killers, Miss Harrington," he spluttered. "You open yourselves up to great peril. Murderers will stop at nothing to hide their sins!"
"I know, Inspector, and in future, we will be more careful. But can you tell me if Agatha named her killer?"
She heard a sound that resembled snarling. "No. More's the shame. That would have been case closed. We're still

processing the scene so perhaps we'll find something else that reveals who it is."

"Well, thank you for calling, Inspector. Let us know if there's *anything* we can do."

"I think we can—oh! There is. Blast it! I set up an evaluation with Pierre Ancien tomorrow morning at his shop and asked that Wainright fellow to come along too. I'm sending Hargrove in my place but…"

"You'd like us to go?" In his present state of mind, he did not need to know that Pierre had already told them and they were planning to be there anyway.

"Would you? Hargrove's a decent sort but not too good with details. I need a level head there, or a couple." It was an attempt to lighten the dark mood.

"You can count on us, Inspector."

She replaced the telephone receiver with a less than steady hand.

"Hot crumpets!" wailed Imogen. "Another murder and it's our top suspect!"

Impeccably dressed as usual, Pierre had substituted his monocle for a tiny eye magnifier. It was the first time the twins had got a really good look at the murder weapon. The hilt was gold, inlaid with a large ruby, a smaller emerald and a sapphire which together, shone in the light of the lamp on Pierre's desk. The cross guard was also jeweled, the ends scrolled downward.

The small office was crowded with Pierre, Algernon, the twins and the constable.

Pierre looked up, removing the magnifier. "Priceless. In my professional opinion the knife is well over four 'undred years old. It is worth a small fortune."

"Brought here during the Dissolution of the Monasteries," croaked Algernon, nodding his head sagely.

"It was never intended as a weapon," continued Pierre. "Purely ceremonial. You can tell because the blade is gold which is not as sharp as iron. But it did the job, in this case, because it was used with such force. If you look closely, the tip is slightly bent."

They all leaned forward to take a look.

"Can you tell us any more about the transfer of treasure during that time in history?" Imogen asked Algernon.

Hand trembling atop his cane, Algernon took the seat Pierre offered.

"There were over eight hundred monasteries leading up to Henry VIII's separation from the church in Rome. They each had artifacts for the sacrament of the Lord's supper and collections of other religious significance. They owned huge swathes of land too.

"Once the king had set himself up as the head of the new church in England, he ordered most monasteries closed and the wealth transferred. You can imagine how that would upset the monks. According to their teachings, these precious items belonged to God. So, a system of spiriting the treasure away to safe places was created, to prevent them falling into the hands of the crown.

"The treasures stayed just ahead of the king's men. Saffron Weald was one such repository. I have even found writings of people who said that the church here was a safe place for Catholic bishops who were also being hunted as traitors. It is purported that there is a priest's hole hidden somewhere in the church, but no one has discovered it, as far as I am aware."

A priest's hole! That could explain how someone could arrive at the church undetected. *What if it was in the vault itself?*

"I'll take that then, sir," said Constable Hargrove, reaching out his hand for the dagger.

Surrendering the knife, Pierre announced, "I 'ave been asked by the vicar to inventory the entire vault since the ledger Septimus used is missing. I shall advise 'im to secure the treasures by changing the door of the vault to the type used by banks. It is madness to have such wealth ripe for the picking."

"Do you mind if we tag along?" asked Ophelia. The other items on their to-do list could wait. She wanted to get into the vault. "I'll even offer to be your scribe."

"What wonder is this?" breathed Pierre on gaining access to the sacred vault. "This should really all be on display for the whole world to enjoy, Vicar."

"I honestly didn't really comprehend how much it was all worth myself, Pierre. I don't often come down here. But since this ugly business began, I can hardly sleep for worry. I've sent an official letter to my superiors asking for guidance on where to go from here. It would certainly help me sleep again if this were all in some museum under lock and key. If only we could find Septimus's record, I wouldn't need you to do all this, as he was meticulous."

Pierre looked over the treasure much as Aladdin might have gazed on the wealth of the thieves and rubbed his hands together. "It will be my pleasure, Bartholomew."

"I'll leave you to it then."

The dim light of the vault made the close work frustrating for Ophelia, but Pierre didn't seem to mind. Plus, she was anxious to begin her search for the priest's hole. Imogen was currently in the coffin area of the crypt on that particular mission, looking along every wall and into every dark corner. Pierre was so engrossed he did not even notice her absence.

After an hour, Imogen reappeared, festooned with cobwebs and covered in dust. She shook her head.

"Let's swap," Ophelia suggested, handing the new ledger over to her sister. "Your handwriting is better than mine anyway."

Parting a particularly large cobweb that hung from her hat, Imogen gratefully took the book and pencil while Ophelia slithered off to the edges of the vault room.

She ran her fingers along the bottoms of walls, up the sides and across the top of shelves. Moving piles of artifacts, she peered behind them to the bare walls. *Nothing.*

A couple of wooden steps divided the room into two levels and since there were no chairs, she sat on the top one, putting a hand to her aching back and pulling her head to the side to stretch out her neck. Head extended to the right, she opened her eyes and noticed something glinting by the bottom step.

A modern paper clip.

Creeping forward, she wrapped her fingers around the clip and as she did so, discovered a crack in the wooden step. Dragging her finger along the split in the wood, she stopped.

A breeze.

The nerves in her fingers definitely registered a movement of air.

Popping the clip into the pocket of her cardigan, she pushed against the cracked side of the step.

To her surprise, the panel swung down revealing a long, narrow hole about eighteen inches high. Lying flat on the ground, Ophelia rolled herself into the opening, yelling as she fell about four feet, landing in the dark on a bed of old, musty hay.

"Imogen! Pierre!"

The shuffle of shoe soles on the stone above told her they were moving.

"Where are you?" asked Imogen with concern.

"Down here. By the steps."

The sliver of dim light was blocked as Imogen found the opening. "Clever you!"

"Bring a torch! It's pitch black down here."

Pierre handed his torch to Imogen who dropped it into the hole.

As Ophelia swung the light she gasped. "There's a low passage. Come down with me. I want to see where it leads."

"There is no way I can squeeze through that 'ole," declared Pierre. "I'll stand guard at this end."

Imogen laid herself on the cold, hard floor and rolled, just as Ophelia had done, landing with a thud. "Ouch!" She got to her feet but could not stand upright in the shallow space. "I'm getting too old for this kind of thing, lovey."

"Don't be silly. Follow me." Ophelia led, shining the beam of the torch ahead.

"I hope the batteries don't run out before we find the exit," whispered Imogen. "We've been using the torch upstairs for some time."

"Be positive," reprimanded her sister as they half crawled along the low, earthy passage.

"How did you discover it?" asked Imogen.

"Sheer accident. I sat down on the step because I was fed up and found a small clip on the floor by the stair. When I reached for it, I felt a breeze and rubbed my fingers along a crack and voila."

Large and small roots had penetrated the ceiling of the tunnel over the years, the small ones trailing along their faces, making Imogen's skin crawl. She was beginning to feel the slightest bit claustrophobic and hoped the passage would end soon.

"How far do you think we've come?"

"It's hard to tell," replied Ophelia as they inched along.

Just when Imogen could take the confinement no longer and was about to scream, a ray of light appeared. Ophelia hurried on and looked up through a small, rusty metal drain. A pool of water had created a muddy puddle beneath it in the tunnel.

"Oh, dear. Our shoes are going to get ruined," Imogen lamented.

"It's all in the name of justice, ducky."

Ophelia pushed on the grating which gave way easily and pulled herself up, looking around. "You'll never guess where we are!"

Imogen reached her arms through and elbowed her way up.

"The haunted house!"

Chapter 23

Centuries before the twins were born, a small cottage, a little removed from the village center, had gained the reputation for being haunted. The legend was that a man had murdered his young wife in the dwelling on their wedding night and in anger and torment she spent eternity haunting the place. Over the intervening years, the folktale had taken on a life of its own. By the time the twins were old enough to understand what ghosts were, a huge tree had grown up in the center of the cottage and rammed through the roof. The surrounding trees and bushes had swarmed into a tangled web that surrounded the exterior like an angry mob.

These days, the only time anyone ventured near the cottage was on a dare. Even then, the youths were so terrified of running afoul of the angry ghost, they only ever entered the front garden. Never the cottage itself.

The drain the twin sisters had found was just outside the fortress of bushes at the back of the forlorn and forgotten property. The abandoned cottage was the perfect spot for a priest to remain undiscovered.

Standing in the sunlight, Ophelia's shoulders shuddered, eyes streaming as she pointed a finger at her sister. In turn, Imogen studied Ophelia's appearance and a smile tugged at her lips. They were both covered in dirt and muck from the tunnel. Imogen began to brush her speechless sister down as clouds of dust fell from her dress.

"We look like a couple of vagabonds," giggled Imogen as Ophelia did the same for her.

Finally able to speak, Ophelia wheezed, "You know what this means?"

"The thief could enter the church through the tunnel without being seen," declared Imogen. "Which is why no witnesses ever saw them. But wouldn't they be filthy?"

Ophelia clasped her hands under her chin. "We got it wrong. *We* thought the cassock was for disguise but now I believe it was used to keep the dirt off the thief's clothing and hair which is why it was stashed in the crypt and why it needed a hood."

"My dear, you are a genius."

"And we forgot a clue while we were hypothesizing last night—remember that dusting of dirt on the floor that Septimus accredited to a rat? I suggest that there was no rat at all. The dirt fell from the thief when they removed the monk's habit. That's why Septimus kept having to sweep."

They replaced the grill and walked back to the church chattering about what this meant for the case.

"Someone discovered the priest's hole by accident, someone who needed money," began Ophelia. "It was well known that Septimus was in charge of the vault treasures but possibly not as well known how fastidious a record keeper he was. Anyone who saw the amount of treasure in there would never imagine that anyone would notice a few things missing."

Imogen chopped the air with her hands. "But on that fateful day, Septimus must have been in the crypt at an unexpected time and come upon the thief who panicked and picked up the closest weapon to hand."

"Yes!" declared Ophelia in agreement. "We now know the how and part of the why. We just need to find the who."

By this time, they were back at the church where they found Pierre sitting by the open priest's hole.

"You look like a pair of ragamuffins," he grinned, an arm resting on his knee. "Glad I was too big to make it through the 'ole. Tell me, what did you find?"

"Are you familiar with the haunted cottage?" asked Imogen.

Pierre had moved to the village twenty years ago and was still considered a newcomer. The lines between his eyes relayed his incomprehension. They filled him in on the legend.

"So, the priest would bolt down the 'ole and 'ide out in the old cottage?" he asked.

"Possibly, or just stay put in the tunnel. It's pretty clever. I think I learned in school that the whole notion of priest's holes was the idea of one Jesuit priest."

"Bravo!" He broke into another heart stopping grin, then got to his feet. "Well, as exciting as recording all these artifacts is, I think we 'ave done enough for today. And you two need a bath."

♪

They had just cleaned up when a knock came at the door sending Tiger into paroxysms of barking.

"Inspector! Come in." A traveler could pack quite well for a week in Paris using the bags under the poor man's raw eyes.

Upon learning that the stranger was actually a friend, Tiger stopped his noise and trotted into the living room. Ophelia followed with the inspector in tow.

"Can we get you some coffee? You look done in," asked Imogen.

"That would be lovely," he groaned.

"I've come to see what you can tell me about the dagger?" he said, while Imogen was making his drink. "I couldn't get a hold of Mr. Ancien."

"Oh, Inspector Southam! We have far more valuable news than the worth of the dagger. We just found a secret passage used by priests in the 1500s."

Even without the jolt of energy from a cup of coffee, the inspector's face broke open. "Tell me more."

As Ophelia explained their exploits, Imogen returned with a warm cup and a biscuit.

The inspector took a sip with closed eyes. "Well, I never. So, you think the cassock was used to keep them clean in the underground tunnel, you say?"

"We believe so. I remember Septimus telling us he thought they had mice as he was constantly finding a dusting of dirt on the floor. At the time, I paid little attention to his comment, but with this new information, it seems obvious that it was the thief shaking off the dirt before emerging from the crypt. We're planning to call the dramatic society this evening to ask if they're missing a cassock from their wardrobe."

"As for the dagger," Imogen continued. "Pierre said it is priceless. He also noticed that it was slightly bent at the very tip. He explained that it is a ceremonial dagger, not one intended for violence, and that it was made of pure gold which is a softer metal. Algernon confirmed his deduction and told us about the history of the treasure and then mentioned the rumor that a priest's hole had been built into the church."

"Well, I couldn't resist after that," declared Ophelia, eyes twinkling. "It was a challenge."

She waited until the exhausted man had drained his cup before asking about the second murder. "What can you tell us about Agatha's death, Inspector?"

"Not much. Like I said, she was strangled with one of her own scarves, but we found no clues other than the discarded attempts at the blackmail letter."

"If you recall, Agatha was in dire need of money. You must have noticed the smell of mold in her cottage. It's because her roof leaks like a proverbial sieve. It was becoming a health hazard. And I would guess that she had run out of things to pawn so blackmail must have seemed like a good idea."

"Blackmail is never a good idea," blustered the inspector. "Either Miss Trumble witnessed something incriminating the day of the murder that she later realized revealed the identity of the killer, or she saw something *after* the murder that linked someone to it. I wish she had come to me instead of taking matters into her own hands. She might still be alive."

"And are we to understand that you have not yet found Septimus's ledger?"

"No. That little item is still rather elusive."

Ophelia leaned forward. "*We* had an idea to try and locate it. If we could gain access to something from Septimus's cottage, let Tiger sniff it, then take him on visits to those without alibis, he might be able to lead us to the ledger."

After a brief pause, the inspector said, "At this point, I'm willing to try anything, though if I were less tired, I would probably caution you against confronting someone who has already killed twice."

"We'll be extremely careful, Inspector," Imogen assured him. "And we'll have Tiger to keep us safe."

Southam rubbed his eyes. "I also came here to ask you to set up a drop with the dodgy pawnbroker for half past eleven this evening. Can you do that? The blackmail letters confirm that

Miss Trumble was killed by the same person who stabbed Septimus. I'm hoping that under pressure this slippery pawnbroker will give us a description of the thief he's been working with. Now, I'm going home to get in a few winks but I'll be back this evening."

"Where do you want the meet to take place?" asked Ophelia.

"Ah, yes. Where do you suggest?" asked the inspector. "You know the village better than me."

"How about the haunted cottage? No one else will dare go near it and we could be sure of complete privacy."

"Alright then. I'll get some of my men to hide in the undergrowth and I'll be in hiding too. We'll plan to surround the broker as the buy takes place and make the arrest when he offers you the money. Can you whistle?"

The twins frowned and Ophelia responded. "I can whistle like a bird."

"Splendid! If at any time before the purchase takes place you feel in danger, just whistle and we'll come running. I will be in place well before half past eleven so we can test the whistle before the broker arrives. I'll whistle back so you know I'm there."

"We'll need something to offer him. Something real from the vault. He may be slimy, but he was no fool."

"I'll let you sort that out with the vicar." He struggled to his feet. "Right! My bed is calling." He doffed his hat. "Good day."

As soon as the inspector left, they called Matilda at her shop.

"I know this is a very strange question," began Ophelia, "but could you check the drama society wardrobe to see if you are missing a monk's cassock?"

"I won't be able to go until after I close at five. Is that too late?" asked Matilda.

"That should be fine. Could you also write up a list of people who are members of the Dramatic Society?"

"Is all this anything to do with poor Agatha? I can't believe it. She was a pillar of the community and a personal friend."

"In a roundabout way, yes," admitted Ophelia.

"Then I shall be happy to help you in any way I can."

Once Ophelia had replaced the receiver, Imogen handed her the card from the pawnbroker.

"Yes?" The memorable, scratchy voice came down the line, stringing out the middle of the word.

Ophelia introduced herself as Miss Swithins and reminded him that they had been into their shop the day before.

"Ah, yeah. You had an interesting item to sell, if I recall." Even his speech was slow.

"It is about that very item that I am calling. Would you be able to meet me in Saffron Weald tonight at half past eleven in the garden of an abandoned cottage?"

"Saffron Weald?" His tone had an edge.

"Is that a problem?"

"I daresay not. It's just that I've done business there recently with another party and I don't like to show up in the same place too often. Increases the risk. What is the item?"

"I'd rather not say, if you don't mind. But I can tell you it will be worth your while." She hoped his greed would overshadow his concerns.

"'Ow much are you wantin'?"

"I would say £50 would be a fair price."

"I ain't bringin' any more," he warned.

"Indeed." She gave him directions and times and replaced the receiver. She looked up at Imogen with energy shining from her eyes. "It's all set."

♪♪

The Saffron Weald library was quite full of people buzzing about the second murder. Celina looked worn out.

"Can we have a quick word?" asked Ophelia.

"I'm past due for my break." She took out a sign from her drawer that said, *Be Back Soon,* and bid them follow her through a small door that led to a miniscule office. There were only two chairs, so Ophelia stood.

"I don't know what is happening to this village," Celina said, fine lines marring her youthful skin. "I was due to talk with Agatha tomorrow about a book sharing project between the library and the school and now…" Her voice cracked.

"Actually, we are here on a slightly different matter," said Imogen. "It appears that Septimus was withdrawing books by Shakespeare because he was in love."

Celina's face screwed up into a question. "Septimus?"

"Yes. He extracted phrases and collated them into love letters." She waited for this information to sink in. "Agatha thought he was in love with her."

A look of fear replaced the wonder on Celina's face. "Is that why she was killed?"

"It does not appear so."

"Then why are you telling me?"

"Because it was *you* Septimus was taken with."

If the young librarian had not been sitting, Imogen was sure she would have fallen to the floor.

"You had no idea?" asked Ophelia, though the truth was stamped all over the librarian's features.

"Septimus was old enough to be my father! I never saw any indication..." She paused. "Wait. He had got into the habit of walking with Agatha and I to the church door after choir practice. I thought he was just being a gentleman, but now..."

"Did he ever talk to you about Shakespeare when he borrowed the books?"

"I'm usually pretty busy, but viewing my interactions with him through this lens, he *did* try to engage me in conversation each time he checked out a book. But he was always interrupted by other patrons." Her face collapsed with sadness. "I feel bad about it now, but he was an irritation to me as I had work to do. I didn't really pay him any attention."

The sisters explained how the misunderstanding with Agatha had occurred.

Imogen reached a hand across the desk. "At least she will never know she was not the object of his admiration."

Celina brought to mind a lost child.

"Is there someone who could help you with the library today? Or perhaps you could just close early?" suggested Imogen.

"Yes," Celina murmured. "That might be best."

Ophelia sprang into action and bolted out of the little office.

"Can I have everyone's attention, please," she shouted. "The library is closing for the day. Please reshelve your books and come back tomorrow. We're sorry for the inconvenience."

After a few mutterings, the group of patrons left and Ophelia turned the sign on the door to *Closed*.

After seeing Celina to her home, which was currently a room in someone else's house, they took a detour home to pick up Tiger and made their way to the vicar's.

His color was much better when he opened the door. "Ladies, I hope the choir is ready for the funeral." Tiger strained forward to smell the vicar and Imogen pulled him back.

Today was Wednesday. Choir practice was tomorrow and the funeral on Friday.

"We will have our practice tomorrow, Vicar. Douglas is very capable so I'm sure we'll be well prepared."

He tipped his head and furrows appeared across his brow.

"Oh, yes. Uh - we were hoping to get into Septimus's cottage again. The inspector has agreed to let Tiger smell an item of Septimus's clothing in the hopes of sniffing out that elusive ledger."

He lifted a finger. "Of course. One moment."

While the vicar was gone, his son appeared and grabbed the ball that was tucked under the occasional table in the entryway. Seeing Tiger, he came to the door. "Can I pat him?"

"Yes, if you're gentle," said Imogen.

He reached for Tiger who met him halfway and licked his hand causing the boy to giggle.

"Daddy, can't we get a dog?" he pled when his father returned with the key.

The vicar's demeanor changed to exasperation. "We've had this conversation so many times and you know my feelings on the matter. Now, off with you."

The boy ran past them and out into the driveway, sulking.

"He's welcome to come over any time and play with Tiger. In fact, we would welcome it," said Imogen, ruffling Tiger's fur. "I think he gets bored with just us two old ladies."

"I might just take you up on that. I have severe allergies to dogs, I'm afraid. Here's the key. Just slip it under the mat when you return as I am off on a pastoral visit."

"We also need an artifact from the vault for a police operation," added Ophelia.

Reverend Cresswell quirked a brow.

"You can call Inspector Southam to confirm. We can't tell you about it because it is classified."

He inhaled deeply. "Let me get the other key. I'll get it back from you another time. It goes without saying that you must keep the key and the artifact safe."

As they left the vicarage, Imogen chuckled. "I had half a mind to tell him we didn't need the key to the vault."

Chapter 24

After an eventful trip to the crypt to choose a suitable artifact for the buy that evening, they selected a breathtaking, jeweled chalice. Tiger went completely crackers when introduced to over a century's worth of never-before experienced odors and could only be coaxed out using chunks of smelly cheese.

He was far less impressed with Septimus's pristine cottage that had been cleaned to within an inch of its life by the former occupant, and sat by the front door waiting to leave. Imogen found a blue sweater in a chest of drawers she was sure would hold the deceased verger's scent and waved it under Tiger's nose then offered it to him. Opening his impressive jaws, he took the jumper in his mouth as though it were a sparrow's egg and trotted proudly all the way home. Ophelia carried the golden chalice under her cardigan.

As they opened the door to Badger's Hollow, the peal of the telephone sounded and Ophelia hurried in to answer it.

"Hello. It's Matilda. You were right. We performed *All That's Holy* about five years ago. It's a comedy that features five monks. One of the robes is missing."

"Well, that's one mystery solved," sighed Ophelia.

"If you come by the shop tomorrow, I'll have the list of members ready for you."

Tiger settled into his basket, tucking the shirt under his chin like a blanket as the sisters made a light dinner, though neither was particularly hungry with the shady meet looming over them.

Ophelia practiced the violin to while away the time while Imogen pottered in the garden with Tiger by her side.

At half past ten, dressed totally in black, Tiger by their side, they walked to the haunted cottage. After giving the bird whistle signal, it was returned in kind, assuring them that the inspector and his men were also in place.

The moon was half lit but scudding clouds swept over it at intervals, plunging them into inky darkness. They positioned themselves at the front of the decrepit cottage so that the sinister black marketeer could easily spot their shadows. Tiger could not stand still, unable to settle as if picking up on their nerves. They trusted he would remain quiet since the young gardener had been working on the skill for the last three weeks by gently tapping his snout.

Ophelia checked her watch in the partial moonlight. It was a quarter past eleven with no sign of the weaselly pawnbroker. The priceless chalice was burning a hole in her pocket.

Ten more minutes passed.

Five more.

Suddenly, Tiger tensed, a low growl forming in the back of his throat.

"Here we go," Ophelia whispered.

A dark figure wrapped in black from head to foot approached like a lion stalking its prey. Ophelia fingered the chalice. His face was wrapped in cloth like some Arabian knight, with only the dark, drooping eyes showing. Tiger strained on the lead, growling, and Imogen had to use all her strength to restrain him.

The scoundrel stepped back, anxiety rippling from him. "You didn't say nuffin' about a dog. Is he safe?" The scratchy voice grated.

"You can't expect two old ladies like ourselves to creep about in the middle of the night and not take means to protect ourselves," Ophelia responded tightly.

He remained at a little distance eyeing the dog. "Let's see it then."

Ophelia reached into her pocket, presenting the beautiful cup for viewing.

An instinctive gasp revealed that the pawnbroker appreciated its value. It was obviously worth considerably more than the £50 agreed upon. Greed burned in the formerly lazy eyes.

"Can I 'old it?" He reached a long hand forward.

"Not until I see the money," retorted Ophelia.

Reaching into his pocket the pawnbroker pulled out a roll of banknotes but kept them close. "Now, 'and it over!"

"No. We should exchange goods at the same time," said Ophelia, a quiver in her voice Imogen thought might be genuine. Her own pulse was deafening as she strained to hold the Alsatian at bay.

"Alright." He held out both hands, one holding the money, but as Ophelia mirrored his actions, he swiped the chalice while snatching back the pound notes and turned to flee. Instantly, Imogen released her hold on Tiger. The broker's speed was no match for the dog and within seconds Tiger's fierce jaws were clamped around the thief's forearm, forcing him to drop the chalice to the ground as the air filled with the sound of police whistles and bouncing torch lights. The slippery criminal snapped his head from side to side as Tiger held him firm.

"You set me up!" he whelped.

"Haven't you heard?" said Ophelia smoothly. "There's no honor among thieves."

Inspector Southam stood over the owner of *Vintage Treasures*. "You made the mistake of judging a book by its cover."

Imogen pulled Tiger back and a couple of constables wrestled the odious man to his feet while the inspector cautioned him. The policemen frog marched the broker into the darkness.

The inspector rubbed Tiger's head affectionately. "I could do with someone like Tiger on my force. Well done, boy!" Tiger licked his hand. "We'll let the fellow stew in a cell tonight and hopefully he'll sing like a bird in the morning. I'll let you know if he says anything worthwhile. Good evening, ladies."

Nerves still on double duty, Imogen and Ophelia picked their way across the village.

"There's one important thing I've learned tonight," said Ophelia.

"Oh, yes. And what is that?"

"This dog is worth his weight in gold!"

Chapter 25

Imogen wrestled with sword wielding, desert nomads all night long. She stumbled down the stairs at ten o'clock.

Their systems flooded with pent up nerves and stress, the sisters had giggled most of the way home the night before, flopping around the kitchen table to dissect the events of the evening in minute detail with a warm cup of comforting milk. The clock struck two as they parted ways at the top of the stairs.

"Morning sleepyhead!" exclaimed Ophelia who sported her own set of dark smudges under bleary eyes. "I had the most terrific nightmares. Hardly slept a wink. Reminds me of—never mind."

Tiger perked up.

"Me too!" cried Imogen. "It appears that clandestine meetings with corrupt and felonious men in the middle of the night is not a recipe for uninterrupted slumber."

"Imagine that!" replied Ophelia with a wry smile.

The phone rang.

"I'll get it," said Ophelia. "There's tea in the pot."

She wandered into the hall to the jangle of the bell. "Badger's Hollow."

"It's Matilda. Douglas asked me to call the choir members because he needs to move practice for the funeral to this evening. Gladys is having surgery tomorrow. Can you make it?"

"*If I get in a nap,*" she thought. "Of course."

"And I have that list for you. I'll give it to you at practice. Toodle-loo!"

Hoping that with the pawnbroker's testimony the investigation would be complete, and the murderer revealed, and far too exhausted to do any housework, they waited for a call from the inspector. In the meantime, they pottered around the cottage, played music together, indulging in the occasional catnap in the sitting room.

By the time choir practice drew near, they had heard nothing.

It was a particularly close, late summer evening and as they walked over for choir practice, they looked forward to entering the cool interior of the church.

"Miss Harrington! Mrs. Pettigrew! I am *devastate*d by the news about Agatha." Reggie Tumblethorn was dressed all in black except for a scarlet ascot. "I can hardly believe it. We'll need to prepare to sing at *two* funerals." He fiddled with the scarf at his neck. "A little bird told me Septimus and Agatha were sweethearts. It's like some dark, tragic play from the Middle Ages."

Arabella Fudgeford and Archie Puddingfield entered the church together followed by Prudence Cresswell, who was looking worse for wear.

"Poor Bartholomew. He's really struggling with his sermons for the funerals," she whispered to Imogen. "He's such a sensitive soul."

They all filed into the choir stalls as Douglas came from behind the altar holding a stack of music. "I do appreciate you coming a day early, everyone. We've been hoping for this surgery for Gladys and the doctor had a cancelation tomorrow." He handed out the sheet music as the rest of the choir members joined them. "We'll first observe a minute of silence for dear Agatha."

Imogen tried to observe the expressions around her, but everyone was stoney faced.

"Thank you. Now, let's just give this a run through and look for problems." Douglas arranged his papers on the music stand and tapped the baton. Organ chords surprised Ophelia as she had not seen Matilda arrive.

"Not bad, not bad," Douglas muttered after the first attempt, swinging his hand and accidentally knocking off the papers. He bent to retrieve them. "Matilda! Let's do parts. Sopranos."

By the end of ninety minutes, the piece was ready for the first funeral.

"Thanks everyone," said Douglas gathering up his things. "Take your music home and run through it for Friday. Right, I'm off, then. We have an early start."

As Douglas hurried down the aisle, Matilda approached them with a sheet of paper. "Here's that list. Hope it helps. I don't know what this world is coming to. Tata!"

Reggie came to stand beside the twins.

"Have you sold all your pickled watermelon, Reggie?" Ophelia cast an eye over the list Matilda had handed her. Several members of the choir were listed among the Dramatic Society's members.

"Why? Have you decided to get some?" asked Reggie. "I told you to act quickly. They've all gone."

"All gone?" asked Imogen.

"Yes, every last one. Simon and Douglas came back for more."

There were some things Imogen would never understand.

♫

"I'm going to call the inspector," declared Imogen when they arrived home. "I can't stand it anymore! I know he said he'd call *us* when he had anything to share but I'm dying to know what the pawnbroker said. I don't think it's too late yet."

Once through, she could not hold back. "So? Who sold the pawnbroker the stolen items?"

"Mrs. Pettigrew, I haven't called because the dirty blighter is being tight lipped. He refuses to admit to anything and claims he was just passing by the haunted cottage when he saw movement in the abandoned garden and being a good citizen went to investigate."

"Well, that's ridiculous!" cried Ophelia, listening in. "You caught him red-handed. And he had all that money on him."

"He has an answer for everything, that one," replied the inspector. "Says he has to have cash on him at all times in his line of business."

"What about the chalice?"

"The way he tells it, he heard a noise, went to investigate and found you two ladies with stolen goods. Claims he was leaving to report the crime to the police when your dog viciously attacked him."

"What a despicable man!" choked Ophelia.

"Quite. I'm going to leave him to cook a bit longer and see if he becomes more reasonable. Either way, I've got him on fencing stolen property, I'd just like to mine him for information on our thief and possible murderer. I'll be sure to call if I succeed."

Ophelia's heart sank. "Good night, Inspector Southam."

Chapter 26

Following the disappointment of the day before, Ophelia suggested they occupy themselves by undertaking a little sleuthing. She declared that instead of waiting for Mr. Slimy to spill his guts, they should dedicate the day to a covert search for the elusive treasury ledger. Still using the first murder victim's shirt as a blanket, Tiger was well acquainted with the man's scent.

The high heat of the previous days had dropped and though the sky threatened rain, the weather forecast on the radio assured the public that any liquid sunshine would hold off until teatime. Tiger obediently allowed them to attach his lead, but his tail wagged with ferocious anticipation. Imogen patted a pocket full of doggie treats to encourage compliance.

Eliminating the people who had solid alibis left Patricia Snodgrass, Simon Purchase, Douglas Horton-Black, Desmond Ale, Matilda Butterworth and Celina. They struck the Horton-Blacks off the list since Douglas was with Gladys at the hospital in Parkford.

"Let's start at the post office since the pub won't open for another couple of hours," suggested Imogen.

The cooler weather seemed to tempt the whole village outside. They waved to neighbors in their gardens and children playing outside in the street who stopped to pet the dog. Tiger relished the attention.

Joining the line of people waiting at the post office, Imogen commanded Tiger to sit. Alice Puddingfield was ahead of them, a dusting of flour on the side of her hat.

"Hello, Tiger," she said, rubbing his thick coat. "What a good boy. Can't believe he's the same animal Connie owned."

They explained that the butcher's grandson was training him.

"Well, he's doing a bang up job, I'd say." She dropped her voice. "What's the scoop on Agatha? The paper was very scant on details. According to the colonel, the school governors are having an emergency meeting to appoint an interim headmaster since school will start in a couple of weeks. Dreadful. Simply dreadful."

The twins had read the report in the newspaper too. It had not mentioned the blackmail letters at all. The inspector must have withheld that detail.

"It is truly shocking but according to Inspector Southam her death is not random. It's definitely connected to the death of Septimus," explained Ophelia.

"I don't know if that makes me feel better or worse," Alice muttered. "How could they be connected? Did she and Septimus even really know each other?" She slapped a hand to her mouth. "Was Agatha a witness to Septimus's murder?"

Imogen's eyes flared. "We believe that *may* be the line of investigation the inspector is pursuing."

"And the killer silenced her." Alice shivered. "Are you two helping the inspector again?"

"We are," confirmed Ophelia. "There are certain things little old ladies can accomplish that a man in uniform might have trouble with."

Alice's eyes creased into a smile. "Like questioning me?"

"You and Archie have an alibi, remember?"

"So, you *are* questioning people without them even realizing it," she whispered.

The twins just smiled.

"Do you know, I'm so shaken by all this, my cakes won't rise properly," continued Alice. "My emotional state is affecting the baking process."

"I don't doubt it," said Ophelia as the line moved forward and the vicar's wife joined the end of the queue.

"Good morning." Prudence looked decidedly downtrodden.

"Is everything alright?" asked Alice.

Prudence let out a large puff of air. "As a vicar, one understands that funerals are a difficult part of the job. We accept that. But to have so many in such a short time frame is really taking a toll on dear Bartholomew."

Their vicar was a true Christian man who lived by the tenets of the church. He took seriously his role as shepherd of his flock.

"I can well imagine," said Imogen.

"Septimus's death impacted him on such a personal level. They were great chums, you know. He's quite lost on a Tuesday evening."

"What can I do for you, Alice?" asked Patricia as the customer in front of the baker left.

The twins turned their full attention to Prudence. "I have no doubt the vicar will pay an outstanding tribute to his friend, as will the choir," said Imogen.

"Thank you." She blinked rapidly. "However, considering the facts that Septimus was an orphan and a bachelor, Bartholomew is worried the church will be empty."

"Oh, I don't think he need worry about that!" said Ophelia, counting on human beings' tendency toward morbid curiosity.

"Next!" called Patricia.

"I say, would you mind terribly if I took Tiger back to get a drink? He's rather thirsty." Imogen wore her most innocent expression.

"Uh-I suppose so," said Patricia looking rather taken aback. She walked to the end of the counter and unlocked a panel in it for Imogen before returning to wait on Ophelia who planned to question her at length about her stamps.

Imogen had never entered the living quarters of the post office before. After walking through the sorting room and a supply area, she came to a flight of stairs. At the top was a well-appointed, feminine living room in rose and blue. She removed Septimus's jumper, let Tiger sniff it once more, then put it back in her bag. She guided the dog carefully around the room. Though interested in all the new smells, he did not detect the scent they were interested in.

Moving onto the bedroom, Imogen was momentarily distracted by the beautiful furnishings. Either Patricia had exquisite taste, or she had hired a professional. The dog wandered around the room but did not fix on anywhere in particular.

A small room that was used as an office did not yield results either and she hurried to the kitchen to make it look like she had given the dog some water. Again, letting him roam, the dog did not detect the familiar scent.

Satisfied that nothing belonging to Septimus was hidden in the apartment, she hurried down the stairs where Patricia had launched into the story of how she found a rare Victorian stamp. The line of people was now out the door.

"Thank you so much," Imogen gushed as she joined her sister.

Patricia's story concluded and they paid for their own stamps and some handsome writing paper and convened outside.

Imogen shook her head.

A quick look at the time showed that the public house had just opened.

"I fancy a shandy. How about you?" Ophelia asked Imogen.

"I'd say searching Patricia's flat has worked up a thirst."

They had spent much more time at home negotiating a way to enter Desmond's apartment than Patricia's. At last, they hit upon the fact that the pub had a garden where they could take the dog but no ladies' convenience.

They entered the pub garden with its wrought iron tables and chairs. The space was empty since the pub had not been open for long.

Once they were settled, Ophelia went into the building and ordered two shandies. Desmond was in his usual cheerful mood which she hoped would work in their favor. She carried the two, pint glasses out to the garden. Tiger sat up, sniffing the air.

"Not for you, boy."

The tangy, biting liquid hit the spot and they chatted in low voices about Imogen's visit to the postmistress's living quarters.

After fifteen minutes had passed, Ophelia ran into the pub and in short, loud phrases explained that Imogen had been taken ill. She would definitely not be able to make it home. Might she possibly use Desmond's own facilities for the emergency.

Desmond's bonny countenance clouded in a confusion of embarrassment that he was forced to talk about a lady's digestion in public. "Keep it down, Miss Harrington. I don't want anyone else to hear." He tipped his head. "She can use the back door stairs."

Ophelia skipped out, giving Imogen the thumbs up sign and pointing to the back door. Fortunately, there were still no other customers in the garden and Imogen slipped through the door and up a steep flight of stairs unseen, while Ophelia went back to distract Desmond.

The apartment was old and dated but clean and tidy. She led Tiger around the room noticing wedding pictures and formal portraits of Ale's son in military uniform, thankful that her own son had returned unharmed and that her grandson had been too young to serve.

Moving down the corridor, she found a bedroom that caused her to stop in her tracks. It was a room stuck in the past, a holy shrine dedicated to the memory of a fallen hero. In deference, she decided it was too sacred to disturb.

The next room was obviously Desmond's, but it remained as feminine as the day his wife had died. A rose embroidered bedcover held a silk eiderdown. The walls were a faint pink and the furniture all white pine. Leading Tiger through it, she felt like a trespasser, which of course she was.

The dog did not pick up Septimus's scent and they moved on to a small kitchen, with gleaming, modern appliances. She was admiring an electric toaster and an electric kettle when she heard a door open on the ground floor.

Hot crumpets! Where was the bathroom?

Running back into the hall she noticed a door she had not yet entered and pulled hard. It was a cupboard. *Flamin' heck*! Where was the loo? Eyes darting with panic, she laid eyes on another door and crossing her fingers, dragged Tiger with her. It was the tiniest water closet with barely room for the pair of them.

"Just me, Mrs. Pettigrew," came Desmond's cheery voice. "Just need something from the kitchen. Don't mind me."

Should she groan in pain?

Tiger made a whimpering noise and she tapped him on the nose and slid a treat into his mouth.

"You alright in there?" came the worried voice of the publican.

"Uggh!" she moaned.

"Uh, I'll get your sister." She heard him hammer down the stairs. It had been the right move.

A couple of minutes later, Ophelia tentatively called her name. Imogen opened the door to the W.C. and she and the dog fell out.

"Let's get out of here. I've had enough humiliation for one day," Imogen gasped.

Ophelia pursed her lips while her shoulders shook with mirth and Imogen grabbed her hand, running headlong down the staircase and out into the garden.

Wiping her eyes, Ophelia croaked, "What did you do? Desmond's face was flaming."

"I'd rather not talk about it if you don't mind. And for the record, the missing ledger is not in Desmond's flat."

Leaving Ophelia mute with hysterics, Imogen lifted her nose in the air and stalked out of the beer garden.

Chapter 27

Dressed in formal black for the funeral of Septimus Saville, Imogen and Ophelia bid farewell to Tiger who regarded them with sad eyes. They planned to arrive at the church plenty early to help with any last-minute arrangements and practice the hymn one final time.

The moment they entered, the heady scent of floral arrangements struck them and they gasped as their gazes settled on dozens of elaborate displays on stands in front of the altar.

Other members of the choir were already present, and the vicar was moseying around with a sentimental smile taking over his bland features.

"What a lovely showing!" declared Imogen, thinking of the vicar's worries she had learned from his wife.

"Yes! One of these wreaths is from the diocese, since he was an employee, and others are from members of the village. I can't tell you how touched I am," effused the lanky vicar.

Ophelia wandered over to read the cards. The largest one was from the diocese, as the vicar had mentioned, closely followed in size by a beautiful arrangement from the pub. Other sprays were from the colonel, Douglas, Patricia, and other village inhabitants, as well as their own.

"Everyone in their places!" ordered Douglas, clapping his hands together as he hurried down the aisle clasping the music under his arm. "Is Matilda here yet?"

Matilda Butterworth leaned back from the organ bench. "Present!"

She began to play the hymn as the choir members opened their folders.

"How did it all go?" asked Patricia.

Douglas frowned.

"The surgery?"

"Oh! Splendid! Gladys is resting nicely. I'm headed back to the hospital right after this."

Several more members of the choir arrived, squeezing into their slots.

"Let's go through it once before the congregation arrives." Douglas tapped the music stand and Matilda started from the beginning.

"Lovely," he commented when they were done. "Sopranos, try to sing a little louder now that...your numbers are lower." He stepped down. "I just need a drink. I'll be right back."

Matilda began to play mournful hymns in keeping with a funereal occasion as villagers filed through the entrance to the church. All the shops must have closed for the afternoon in a show of solidarity. Pierre nodded at the sisters as he took his seat. Ophelia glanced at the vicar who was wiping his eyes with a pocket square.

A rush of whispers caused Imogen to look up from her music. Several high-ranking members of the diocese had arrived and by the sappy expression on the reverend's face, they were not expected. He bustled down to lead them to their seats looking both harried and profusely grateful.

Moments later, the pall bearers arrived and the entire congregation stood as Mildred played a dramatic requiem. Once the casket was settled at the front of the church, the assembly sang a hymn and Reverend Cresswell invited the bishop to offer the invocation.

When the bishop was re-seated, the vicar launched into a warm, respectful eulogy, detailing Septimus's life as an orphan through to his faithful service to the church and ending with the deep friendship he and the verger had shared.

Before the benediction, the choir stood as the church fell silent in quiet expectation.

Douglas tapped the music stand, Matilda belted out the opening notes on the ancient organ and the choir plunged into the haunting melody as Douglas swayed, eyes closed while brandishing the baton. As he waved the tapered stick, the tip caught the edge of his music, sending the pages cascading to the floor.

Imogen froze, the notes dying in her throat.

I know what happened!

Chapter 28

Should she cry out? Should she wait? Should she keep singing?

The whole sickening solution to the murder was laid out in Imogen's mind like the plot for a book.

Arabella looked to the side to see why Imogen had stopped singing. Prudence flared her eyes to encourage Imogen to pick up the melody again, but the will to sing had departed.

Imogen stiffened, music in hand, mouth closed, glaring straight ahead.

As the exceptional hymn came to an end, Douglas fashioned a final flourish with the baton, finally opening his eyes to find Imogen's penetrating gaze locked onto his face.

He visibly withered under the menace of her stare.

Ophelia snapped her head toward her sister and instinctively knew what had happened.

The vicar rose to give the benediction but Ophelia cried, "Wait!"

The whole church erupted in hushed, bewildered chatter.

"Wait!" she repeated as the humble vicar hesitated, glancing at his superiors. "I think my sister has something to say on behalf of Septimus before we close."

Imogen's tense jaw now dropped in fright. She was not accustomed to public speaking and she felt her knees go weak. Ophelia pushed through the choir members to support her sister. She squeezed Imogen's hand.

"What better place than at his funeral to unmask Septimus's killer?" she whispered.

Douglas stood rigid, the baton still gripped in his hand.

Imogen cleared her throat. "I know who killed Septimus."

A hushed roaring of whispers swirled around the pillars of the church and up into the rafters.

"It all came together when the sheet music fell," she continued. "I remembered it falling to the floor during practice but I didn't think much of it at the time. But today, I wondered why it kept dropping, and then it hit me. *Because Douglas had lost his music clip.*"

A renewed buzz of incomprehension surged through the sanctuary like a swarm of bees searching for the hive.

Ophelia smacked her forehead. "The clip! The one I found in the crypt by the priest's hole."

"You found a priest's hole?" exclaimed the bishop.

"We did!" declared Ophelia. "It is in the vault and leads to the haunted cottage."

Douglas edged his way off the stand while the crowd was in flux, but Pierre and Fred Fudgeford came up behind him to block his escape. The sound of his knees knocking was almost audible.

"Let's hear it all from the beginning," declared the bishop as the most senior authority in the building.

Ophelia nodded to her sister.

"I believe it all began with an ancient hand-drawn map and the dire need for a special, expensive surgery."

Douglas shrank.

"Years ago, Mrs. Gladys Thornton-Black contracted polio. It cruelly bent her frame causing great pain and forcing her to end a promising teaching career. After consulting doctors for years, I imagine the couple recently learned of a progressive, and probably experimental, surgical procedure that could offer some relief. But it was costly. Outrageously pricey. Where would they get half such a sum?

"Hanging in the Thorton-Black's living room is an antique map of the village. On my last visit to their cottage, I encountered this framed map and discovered that it included a diagram of the church. If I'd had longer to study it, I wager I would have detected the existence of the priest's passage drawn on those plans."

The bishop wheezed.

"This part is an educated guess," continued Imogen, finding her voice. "The Horton-Black's collect first edition books, and

I'm speculating they found the old map between the pages of one of those old tomes. But it doesn't matter where they found it—the salient point is, that they did.

"Douglas must have known of the church's history as a repository for religious treasures during the time of Henry VIII, most of it forgotten. If only he could gain access to the vault, remove some small items no one would notice missing, and sell them to raise money for his wife's surgery. He might have even convinced himself that it was a morally virtuous cause. But how?

"Then he remembered or found the position of the priest's passage in the treasury on the ancient map. Here was the answer. He could enter the vault from the haunted house with no one the wiser.

"However, there was a problem. I know from my own experience that the tunnel is incredibly dirty and Douglas would have been filthy upon exiting. Which would lead to tricky questions.

"But Douglas is a member of the Saffron Weald Dramatic Society. They had performed a comedy a few years before about a group of monks. The monk's habits were roomy and could be worn over clothes and with the hood pulled up, would protect a person from the dirt in the tunnel.

"So, Douglas stole one of the costumes and began accessing the vault through the haunted cottage before choir practice on a Thursday evening and concealing the treasures in the ramshackle cottage to retrieve later. Why on a Thursday? Because he would not have to explain his absence to his wife. The only setback was that he had a narrow window of time. I imagine he would select an item from the treasury, run to hide it in the cottage for later retrieval, return to the vault through the tunnel, remove the dirty cassock, hide it among the heaps of artifacts then emerge from the crypt as if he had been down there to collect his music. It was the perfect plan."

Douglas struggled to escape his captors but they used more force. He was no longer mortified at being discovered, he was furious.

Ophelia beamed with pride.

"Then things went sideways," explained Imogen. "I believe that on the day of the murder, Douglas was exiting the vault and bumped into Septimus. Panicking, he seized the dagger, plunged it in and watched in horror as Septimus succumbed to his mortality. How would he get out of this pickle?

"There was likely blood on him from the attack. He would have to pretend that he found Septimus *already* dead when he went to get his music and got blood on him in his attempt to help the dying man. But he would need more blood to convince people of this scenario, so I think he rubbed some of the blood from the body onto his hands and in doing so, noticed the ledger of church treasures in the pocket of Septimus's jacket. Flicking through, he found notations about the items he had stolen. He *had* to get rid of the ledger too but now it was also covered in blood.

"To further the entire ruse, Douglas faked an injury to appear as if he had passed out in terror. That would muddy the timeline and perhaps swing suspicion away from him. Now, all that was left to do, was run up the stairs feigning shock."

"Liar!" shrieked Douglas while again fighting against his oppressors, and interrupting Imogen's summation.

"Here!" cried Desmond and threw Pierre his tie as a gag. Another person pulled off their tie, which they used to secure Douglas's wrists. Satisfied with their work, they wrestled Douglas onto a pew.

In spite of the interruption, the congregants hung on Imogen's every word, and the bishop himself bid her to continue.

"No one suspected Douglas. We all accepted his version of events. And fortune was with him because the verger had noticed that the thefts occurred around the time of choir practices, so suspicion fell on the other members of the choir. In fact, Septimus believed the robber to be a choir member and had approached my sister and I about helping him uncover the culprit.

"With suspicion turned from him, Douglas relaxed, but stayed well away from the vault."

"What about Agatha?" shouted out Matilda.

"When Douglas appeared covered in blood that evening, wailing that Septimus was dead, Agatha's blood phobia rendered her helpless. Add to that handicap that her heart was broken over the death of her beloved, and she was completely incapacitated."

"Wait!" cried Matilda. "Her beloved?"

Ophelia briefly explained about their pen-pal-style romance.

"She never told me," murmured Matilda.

"The secrecy was part of the appeal," explained Ophelia.

"What does all that have to do with her death?" asked the bishop.

"The combination of shocks damaged her state of mind the night of the murder. Poor Agatha was so debilitated by the combined effect, she was given a sedative by the doctor. It probably wasn't until the next day when she awoke, that she made a connection about the murder that no one else did. And she saw it as a way to solve her own financial problems. Perhaps it was the fact that Douglas stated that he had gone into the crypt to get music from the cupboard but he wasn't holding any, and that the new music we sang from was already on our seats."

"That's right!" declared Prudence. "We began our practice in Doulgas's absence because we had the music."

"And when we rushed down to the crime scene, there was no music on the floor," added Ophelia.

"Well, whatever it was that Agatha figured out, she unwisely used it to blackmail Douglas. Her cottage was falling down around her ears. So she took a risk, and sent him a blackmail note. The police found several practice attempts in her wastepaper bin."

Douglas was growling in spite of the gag, his pale face turning crimson. Apparently, this was a fact he did not know.

"Go on," said the bishop, totally enthralled.

"Now Douglas was boxed in. He could not share the proceeds from his stealing. He needed every bit of that money for the surgery for Gladys. And it was too risky to steal any more artifacts. He would have to silence Agatha. Poor, unsuspecting Agatha."

A sob erupted from Matilda.

Pierre began to clap, then the bishop, then someone else until the whole church exploded with applause.

Chapter 29

As the last haunting notes of the solo violin sonata curled through the leaves of the ancient oak on the village green, the mellow breeze ruffled Pierre's white hair like down feathers.

Imogen had observed Pierre during the performance instead of watching her sister. His focus had been riveted on Ophelia's every movement as she played.

Frozen in time, Ophelia held her position after the last note sounded, like a soft, Michelangelo sculpture.

After thirty seconds, a ripple of applause began and Ophelia separated the bow from the violin and bowed.

Pierre had arranged the musical soirée for the village, and families and couples were spread over the green on blankets as the sun sank below the horizon. It was magical.

As the other villagers gathered up their things, Pierre tenderly pulled Ophelia down to the blanket. Her color was heightened by her impassioned playing, wisps of silver hair that had escaped her bun, forming soft ringlets around her face. The rose pink, crushed silk dress that brushed her ankles and hugged her hips, matched her cheeks. Imogen had the fleeting thought that if she were not there, Pierre would have gathered her sister into his arms and kissed her soundly.

Pierre leaned back supported on one elbow, his legs outstretched. "I still have a few questions."

"Oh?" responded Ophelia.

"Imogen, 'ow were you so sure the killer was Douglas?"

She ran a finger down Tiger's soft nose. "Right before the sheets of music fell off the stand, I looked up from my score and straight into an amber tiepin missing a jewel," Imogen replied. "As the papers spilled onto the floor, it was as though the two images intertwined together in my mind and I knew. Absolutely."

"Alright," said Pierre thoughtfully. "Did the silver embossed lighter belong to Douglas too?"

"Yes. It was as we thought," replied Ophelia. "He used it to light the candles he stole from the worship supply. Gladys identified it right away."

"How did that come to pass?" asked Pierre.

"Inspector Southam turned up at her hospital room and used it to light a cigarette. She told him they had one just like it. That was before he delivered the bad news about her husband."

"Were they in it together?" he asked, pulling up a blade of grass.

"No. Poor Gladys had no idea. He told her he had received an inheritance from a distant relative."

"And the missing ledger?"

"Once they booked Douglas into jail, the inspector sent men to go through their cottage and the gardens with a fine-tooth comb. They found the charred leather remains of the cover in the remnants of a bonfire, but all the pages had burned to ash," explained Imogen.

"So, you will get your wish; to inventory all the treasure in the vault," said Ophelia.

"For an antique enthusiast like me it is a dream come true," he admitted. "To handle objects made by craftsman over four hundred years ago—it's almost as good as falling in love."

Imogen snapped her eyes to his face and Tiger's ears stood on end. Gazing at Ophelia, genuine affection was stamped all over Pierre's features.

"I think I'll take Tiger home. He looks thirsty," she said, getting to her feet. "Coming?"

Ophelia looked at Pierre. "I think I'll stay for a bit…I need to put my violin away."

As Imogen and Tiger crossed the bridge that would take them over the pond and to Badger's Hollow, she stopped and glanced back at the couple under the tree.

Pierre's hand cupped her sister's chin as he leaned toward her.

"Let's go, Tiger. I think we'll raise a glass to second chances."

The End

Thanks for buying my book!

Ann Sutton

I hope you enjoyed book 2, *Church Choirs can be Murder* which is part of a new cozy mystery series I recently created, wrote and published. In case this is the first book you have read of my works there are also two other cozy mystery series I have written that I think you will enjoy – The Dodo Dorchester Mysteries and the Percy Pontefract Mysteries.

The Dodo Dorchester Mysteries is currently an 11-book series.

Book *1* of that series, *Murder at Farrington Hall* is available on Amazon at a special introductory price.

https://amzn.to/31WujyS

"Dodo is invited to a weekend party at Farrington Hall. She and her sister are plunged into sleuthing when a murder occurs. Can she solve the crime before Scotland Yard's finest?"

If you would like a **free** prequel to the Dodo Dorchester Mystery series go to https://dl.bookfunnel.com/997vvive24 to download *Mystery at the Derby*?

The Percy Pontefract Mysteries is currently a 2 book series with book 1, *Death at a Christmas Party: A 1920's Cozy Mystery*, available on Amazon.

https://amzn.to/3Qb4BhG

A merry Christmas party with old friends. A dead body in the kitchen. A reluctant heroine. Sounds like a recipe for a jolly festive murder mystery!

"It is 1928 and a group of old friends gather for their annual Christmas party. The food, drink and goodwill flow, and everyone has a rollicking good time.

When the call of nature forces the accident-prone Percy Pontefract up, in the middle of the night, she realizes she is in need of a little midnight snack and wanders into the kitchen. But she gets more than she bargained for when she trips over a dead body.

Ordered to remain in the house by the grumpy inspector sent to investigate the case, Percy stumbles upon facts about her friends that shake her to the core and cause her to suspect more than one of them of the dastardly deed.

Finally permitted to go home, Percy tells her trusty cook all the awful details. Rather than sympathize, the cook encourages her to do some investigating of her own. After all, who knows these people better than Percy? Reluctant at first, Percy begins poking into her friends' lives, discovering they all harbor dark secrets. However, none seem connected to the murder…at first glance.

Will Percy put herself and her children in danger before she can solve the case that has the police stumped?"

For more information about all my cozy mystery series go to my website at www.annsuttonauthor.com and subscribe to my newsletter to see what I am currently working on.

You can also follow me on Facebook at: https://www.facebook.com/annsuttonauthor

About the Author

Agatha Christie plunged me into the fabulous world of reading when I was 10. I was never the same. I read every one of her books I could lay my hands on. Mysteries remain my favorite genre to this day - so it was only natural that I would eventually write my own.

Born and raised in England, writing fiction about my homeland keeps me connected.

After finishing my degree in French and Education and raising my family, writing has become a favorite hobby.

I hope that Dame Agatha would enjoy the Saffron Weald Mystery series as much as I do.

Acknowledgements

I would like to thank all those who read my books, write reviews and provide suggestions as you continue to inspire.

My proof-reader – Tami Stewart

The mother of a large and growing family who reads like the wind with an eagle eye. Thank you for finding little errors that have been missed.

My cheerleader, marketer and IT guy – Todd Matern

A lot of the time during the marketing side of being an author I am running around with my hair on fire. Todd is the yin to my yang. He calms me down and takes over when I am yelling at the computer.

My beta readers – Francesca Matern, Stina Van Cott

Your reactions to my characters and plot are invaluable.

20BooksTo50K for their support of all indie authors and their invaluable knowledge of the indie publishing world.

Printed in Great Britain
by Amazon